STARFISH GIRL

Athena Villaverde

Eraserhead Press
Portland, OR

ERASERHEAD PRESS
205 NE BRYANT
PORTLAND, OR 97211

WWW.ERASERHEADPRESS.COM

ISBN: 1-936383-30-6

CHAPTER ONE

The starfish girl steps through clusters of furry pink sea sponges, picking out the ones that would make good tampons. Her long black pigtails swing from side to side beneath a starfish that grows from her head like a cute purple hat. She skips within the twilight garden of glowing sea life, squishing jellyfish mushrooms beneath the chunky heels of her black rocking horse shoes. In the aqua sky, yellow-striped sharks circle above the glass ceiling of the underwater dome. The starfish girl sees the sharks reflected in a pool of green squid ink and looks up at them with a big purple smile.

"Pretty!" she says.

Under a swirl-patterned clamshell, the starfish girl finds the fluffiest sponge of the day. She places it neatly into her crabshell purse and clutches it close to her chest. She twirls to inspect her black dress to make sure that it didn't get dirty during the sponge hunt. She takes pride in her outfits and even the tiniest splash of green ink would be heartbreaking. The outfit includes a knee-length jumper dress that bells out from her waist with layers of petticoats and tiny purple bows, a white blouse with puffy sleeves capped with matching purple lace, and purple-striped stockings with little black stars on the ankles. She likes to have purple in everything she wears so that her clothes will match the starfish on her head.

Finding not a trace of dirt on her clothing, the starfish girl decides to seek out a nice place to have a picnic. She leaves the sponge garden and skips through the seashell-paved city street. Buildings webbed with bright green seaweed line the road. Spiky blue urchin trees dot every corner. The city is beautiful to the starfish girl. She thinks it is sad nobody lives here anymore.

While skipping from urchin to urchin, the starfish girl hears a loud metallic scratching noise. The tips of the starfish on her head point upward in alert. She wonders if the city isn't completely deserted after all. Curious to make new friends, she skips in the direction of the sound.

She follows the noise around a corner to discover buildings coated in glowing yellow algae. The starfish girl freezes mid-skip. She takes a step back. Her parents always warned her never to go near the yellow algae, no matter how pretty she thought it was. The stuff is worse than poison. Still, the starfish girl is curious about the noise and doesn't think a little skip through the yellow street would do any harm.

The building where the metallic sounds come from is just down the block. When the starfish girl comes to the entrance, she sees clacking metal crab claws and ducks behind an algae-coated rock. Inside, there are several crabmen, prying into an iron septic tank to feed on the human waste within. The men have angry red faces and yellow eyes. Their muscles bulge under their tight black t-shirts like body builders.

One of them has a tattoo of an anchor on his shell. The man next to him has one giant mechanical claw for one arm and a short deformed fleshy claw for the other. A third crabman with six articulated legs adjusts the gears in his telescope eye and a bright red laser beam shines onto the girl's purple starfish cap as she peeps out from behind the rock.

The crab men back away from the septic tank and turn their attentions toward the girl. Metal Claw snarls at her and snaps his giant pincher. A puff of steam comes out the top of his elbow where the machinery joins his flesh. Telescope Eye targets her with his laser beam. He grins a wide pointy-toothed grin, his crab skin hard as armor, he exposed parts of his flesh spiky and covered with coarse hair.

The starfish girl runs, flouncy skirt bobbing up and down. She slips on a patch of yellow algae as she darts across the street, regains her footing and continues on, keeping her purse tight to her chest. Looking back over her shoulder, she sees the mutants snapping their monstrous claws after her. Her breath quickens, the salt air stings her lungs. She turns another corner. The sound of scuttling crab feet, tick-tick-ticking on the pavement, grows louder.

A sharp cramp in her abdomen causes the girl to cringe and pause for a second. Metal Claw catches up to her. His girl-sized pincher is rusted and covered in sea mussels. He lunges sideways and snaps the jagged-edged claw at her. It snags her dress and tears off one of her purple bows as she jumps away from him. She runs, the rubber ribbons in her pigtails fluttering behind her. The heels of her rocking horse shoes make a clacking sound against the ground that echoes down the hollow alleyways.

She glances back again to discover that she has gained

a bit of distance, but the crabmen do not give up their pursuit. The sound of their hard shells tapping the ground pounds her eardrums. She tears down seaweed vines to get through a narrow corridor that leads to a steep staircase. She climbs.

Halfway up, the steps become slimy with algae. Her foot slips, she loses balance and falls forward. Her knees scrape against the hard edge of the stair. Using her hands to break the fall, the crabshell purse drops from her embrace and tumbles through the air. As she reaches out for it, the heel of her shoe slips on the wet algae again and she slides backward down the steps, just as the crabmen reach the bottom of the stairs.

The tattooed crab raises a claw into the air and drools at her. Two of the crabmen scuttle over each other to fit up the narrow stairway. The girl reaches out in all directions, searching for something to grab onto to stop her fall, but her fingers slip across the yellow railing and she topples downward. The bell of her dress poufs out and her arms get tangled within the multi-layered petticoat.

As her hip bangs against the bottom step, she shakes her pigtails out of her eyes to discover an orchestra of crab claws clicking in her face. Just before they close in on her, a red figure summersaults overhead. It lands between her and the attackers. The starfish girl looks up to see a woman standing before her. The woman has red and white-swirled skin, wears patchwork eel-skin clothing, and has sea anemone hair.

The strange woman looks down on the starfish girl through her chili pepper-red dreadlocks and says, "Get lost."

The starfish girl hops to her feet and crawls up the stairs

on all fours with her fluffy butt in the air. At the top of the staircase, she watches the black leather clad woman toss her head and her sea anemone tentacles swing around her body releasing dozens of crimson darts. Like harpoons they fly at the crabmen, knocking them backward. Three of the crabmen look down to discover darts in their chests, injecting them with a pink fluid. A stinging sensation spreads through their crabshells and they fall to the ground, paralyzed.

Before the other crabmen can regroup, the sea anemone woman drives her tall black leather boot square into Metal Claw's chest plate. He flies backward into the others and they fall in a tangle of legs and claws through the corridor. Metal Claw's massive frame slams against the tattooed crabman, cracking both of their shells down the middle.

The starfish girl's eyes light up as the woman spins like a parasol, swinging her tentacles in graceful arcs. They slice through crabmen on her left and right. Blood sprays through the air, raining down in thick goopy drops, splattering across the seashell ground. It's a wild dance. Her undulating body breaks through a stream of water dripping from a pipe, and the spray of droplets reflect the red of the blood and the red of her anemone hair.

The crabmen scream. Some of them try to flee, but they have been frozen in place by her poison darts. The red swirl-skinned woman walks forward with cat-like footsteps, drawing an infinity sign with her head, causing her whip-like hair to sweep in front of her from right to left with crackling intensity.

The crabman with the laser sight in his eye trips over the jagged edge of Metal Claw's bloody broken shell as he runs away. He falls on his back, his six legs flailing in the air above him, the soft center of his abdomen exposed. The woman does an aerial cartwheel. Her tentacle dreads slice through the remaining two crabmen as she plants the heel of her boot into the supine crabman's stomach. His exoskeleton breaks and her foot sinks into his chest up to mid-calf.

"Repulsive little insects," the woman says, looking down at her mutilated victim. His claws twitch as he takes his last breath.

She pries her foot out of his now sticky demolished body and stomps firmly on the ground in order to knock his blood and viscera off of her boot. Her shoulders roll back and she takes three long slow steps, crushing the tiny heads of the three paralyzed crabmen. Then she gathers mechanical implants from the corpses, ripping them out of their exoskeletons and placing them into a fishnet bag. Stringy crabmeat drips from the netting as she flings the bag over her shoulder.

The sea anemone woman retrieves the crabshell purse from the bottom of the stairs and walks up to the girl. The points on the girl's starfish hat curl up slightly as the sea anemone woman holds out the purse. The girl takes it and bows with a nod of her head.

"You're nice," says the starfish girl.

The woman glares at the yellow algae smudged across the girl's black lolita dress. "I'd clean that stuff off if I were you." The woman then turns on one heel and starts walking away. "Unless you want to end up like them."

As the woman leaves the corridor, the starfish girl looks down at her yellow-blotched dress. Then the points of her starfish shoot upward as she gets an idea. Opening her crabshell purse, she retrieves a handful of fluffy pink sponges and wipes them against her dress until all of the yellow is gone. Her glossy purple lips curl into a smile as the last bit of yellow disappears, but then her smile turns to a frown as she comes to the realization that her favorite of the pink sponges has been ruined by the toxic gunk.

She straightens her bows and petticoats, and tries to hide the tear in her hem. Her rocking horse shoes clack-clack down the steps as she runs after the sea anemone woman.

As the starfish girl catches up to her, the woman stops midstep, her bag of metal parts dripping with fishy oils. The girl inches backward.

"Where do you think you're going?" the woman says, smoothing out one of her tentacles of hair.

The starfish girl says, "I'm looking for nice people."

Then she bows her head and reveals the shimmering pink spots on the top of her starfish.

"There's no nice people here."

The woman walks away, down the street, the sound of seashells crushing beneath her black stiletto heels.

The starfish girl waits until the woman turns the corner. She straightens the strap of her crabshell purse on her shoulder, twirls one of her pigtails between her fingers, and then sneaks after her.

CHAPTER TWO

The metal body parts inside of the fishnet bag leak droplets of oily blood, leaving a trail behind the sea anemone woman as she heads toward a cluster of buildings up ahead. She's unaware of the girl following her, too absorbed in her surroundings, surprised by what a dump this place has become. Most of the windows on all of the buildings have broken and seashell doors have fallen off their hinges. Long cords of seaweed cable litter the ground and everything stinks like a vaginal infection.

The starfish girl sees an amethyst snail crawling along one of the bone-white buildings. She tugs gently on its shell until it comes off the wall with a *POP*. Placing it into her palm, she giggles as its purple slime tickles her skin.

"Cute!" she says to the snail.

The anemone woman hears the girl and turns around to face her.

"Where are we going?" asks the girl, the points of her starfish turning sideways.

The woman's eyes narrow as she glares.

"Your hair is really pretty," the starfish girl says. "Your

head is like a flower."

The woman shifts her dripping bag to the other shoulder.

"Go back to your parents."

The girl's eyes turn back to the snail.

"My parents are dead."

The woman bites one of the hoop piercings on the side of her red-lined lip. Then she says, "Yours and everyone else's," before turning around and continuing on her way.

The girl follows after her and says, "My name's Ohime."

"Good for you."

The girl walks alongside her, looking up at the woman's wild flowery hair.

"It's my birthday today."

The woman rolls her eyes. "Great."

"I'm fifteen now."

"Congratulations."

The woman picks up her pace and heads toward the section of city that is actually inhabited. A disheveled flounder man is sprawled across the puke-stained pavement, snoring mechanically, bubbles foaming out of his mouth. She comes to a doorway with a glowing blue sign above it that reads "The Salty Hag." As she pushes open the door, her heel squishes the flounder man's wrinkled fin between two seashells in the pavement. He grumbles in his sleep, farts, and rolls over, tearing away the top of his withered fin. The flap of fish flesh sticks to the bottom of her stiletto like a piece of toilet paper as she enters the bar.

The starfish girl waits outside, playing with her snail. She likes the way it makes purple slimy spider-web designs along her skin as it crawls up her arm.

***

Inside the bar, a network of glass tubes laces the ceiling. Thousands of blue luminescent fish swim through the tubes, lighting the room. The woman's red-swirled skin turns a pale purple as she enters the blue glow. A dolphin man with a black pompadour hairstyle wearing chainmail suspenders over a white wife beater is tending bar. His left shoulder is made of brass and creaks like it's in need of oiling as he wipes down the clamshell counter with a dirty white rag. He raises his eyebrows at her. She can't tell his true expression because his elongated face gives him a permanent smile.

"What the hell are you doing here, Timbre?" says the dolphin man. "I thought I told you never to come back here."

"I've got some stuff for you," she says, walking over to him.

"You better not kill another one of my customers," he says. "Customers are hard to come by these days, ever since the yellow algae hit this region."

"That guy deserved what he had coming to him." Timbre heaves her oily bag of parts onto the bar.

"What's this shit?" the dolphin man says, eying the heap of junk.

"Spare parts."

She spreads the contents of her bag out on the table. There's the laser sight, the metal claw, an assortment of twisted gears and some small silver ball bearings. The bartender inspects each piece carefully. He twists the clockwork of the gears and holds the laser sight up to his left eye.

"What do you want for them?" he asks.

The woman stares into his beady dolphin eyes, smoothing one of her tentacles with a red-painted fingernail.

"A thousand credits and a dome map."

"A thousand credits?" he says. "You've been getting into too much yellow algae. You've got to be crazy if you think this crap is worth that."

"Fine, I'll take them somewhere else."

"I'll give you three hundred."

She starts putting the pieces of metal back into the bag.

"Okay, take it easy," he says, putting his hand on top of the laser sight before she can remove it from the bar. "Five hundred."

She pries his fingers off the laser and then puts it in the bag with the rest of the parts.

"Hey," he says, "that thing isn't even working. It will need complete rewiring. I'll give you six hundred. That's my final offer."

"And a dome map."

"What the hell do you need a map for?"

"I need to get to the other side of the dome—Ghoshi Territory."

He laughs. "A map's not going to help you, honey." He wipes the oily blood off the bar where the parts had lain. "Not in Ghoshi Territory. Not anywhere. There's not a single piece of terrain under the dome that's recognizable since the collapse."

Her red fingernail taps hard against the clamshell surface of the bar. "The roads are still intact."

He realizes that she's serious. He starts to draw a beer from the tap. Then he asks, "Why the hell do you need to go to Ghoshi Territory anyway? Nothing's out there."

"I heard about some rich guy. Before the collapse, he blew his wad on a private bunker filled with supplies, food, weapons, the works. The guy didn't realize the yellow algae growing outside his kids' bedroom window and they mutated fast, crazed with hammerhead shark DNA. The little fuckers got to him before he ever had the chance to make use of the bunker. Now it's just there, waiting for me."

"Sounds like a load of manatee shit."

"We'll see. So do we have a deal?"

"Yeah, sure."

A large sea bass man at the end of the bar grunts, and the bartender serves him a bowl full of rotting fish guts.

Timbre glances out the window and sees the starfish girl still outside. The girl places her snail on the sleeping flounder man's forehead and it draws purple slimy spider-web designs across his bald scalp like hair. Then she takes some seashells out of her crabshell purse and lays them on top of the man's chest. The woman wonders how such an innocent and helpless girl is still alive after all that's happened.

The bartender rummages through a pile of water damaged papers under the counter of the bar and sorts through them. Then he passes Timbre a crinkled up map. She unfolds the warped yellowed paper and inspects the mess of squiggles and lines.

"Know where I can pick up a hydro-bike?" she asks.

"Supplies are really scarce these days, transportation even more so. The entire market has almost collapsed just in this past week. Things are really grim. But you might try your luck in La Boca, about three miles west of here."

He points to the location on the map.

"Thanks, I'll check it out." She stands there, staring at him.

The bartender pours a pint of beer and puts it in front of her. She ignores it.

"Kelpie Ale?" he asks, pointing at the beer. "Half price."

"I'm still waiting for those six hundred credits." She pushes the beer back.

His dolphin smile is unchanged.

"Yes, yes of course," he fumbles with his wallet, his brass shoulder creaking and rattling like it's about the fall apart at any minute and then hands her the cash. "Now get the fuck out of here."

"Whatever," she rolls her eyes at him and walks out of the bar.

***

Outside the Salty Hag, the tips of Ohime's starfish perk up as Timbre steps back over the flounder man. She notices the fishnet bag is now empty of its contents. Timbre turns down an alleyway to the left of the bar and Ohime follows her, abandoning the snail on the man's head.

"I thought I told you not to follow me," says Timbre without turning around.

Ohime follows her.

Timbre inhales through her nose. "You don't want to die on your birthday, do you?"

Ohime's violet eyes widen. "But you're nice. I'm looking for nice people."

The sea anemone woman exhales. "I will cut your head off."

"The dolphin man in there said your name is Timbre. I like that. It's a pretty name."

The sea anemone woman grinds her teeth and walks away. The starfish girl sticks by her side, not able to take the hint.

CHAPTER THREE

Timbre hears a loud explosion behind her and turns around to see that the back door has been blown off the Salty Hag. Shards of glass litter the alley and little glowing blue fish flop around on the ground. She looks over at Ohime, who is bending down with cupped hands trying to scoop up one of the little fish.

Timbre hooks Ohime by the waist with her right arm and leaps behind a trash can. She peeks around the side—her tentacles straightening to points—to see a tall lanky man exit the doorway. The man has the head of a Moray eel. His skin is red with white spots and he has two large yellow eyes on each side of his face that blink through a mechanical skull cap. He drags a short plump man from the bar out into the alleyway. The man screams as the eel shoves him against the wall and clamps his large jaw around his head.

The eel man's jaws tear the plump man's head off with a *crack*. He looks over his left shoulder and Timbre follows his gaze to a shadowy figure standing at the end of the alleyway near the front entrance to the bar. The figure steps out of the darkness: an obese man in a shiny silver suit, his skin covered in barnacles like a plague victim. He puffs on a seaweed-wrapped cigar and blows rings of smoke from his blistered gray lips.

"What the hell is Dr. Ichii doing here?" she whispers.

Two more figures emerge from the blown out back door. One is a blue woman with a roosterfish fin mohawk on her head, the other a grey-skinned shark man with a circular saw blade implanted on his back where a dorsal fin would be. The pair of them are covered in blood. The woman has a handful of intestines dangling from her fist trailing back to a body lying in the entryway. It's the bartender.

The mohawk woman pulls on the intestine cords and the dolphin man's body gets dragged through the doorway into the alley. Timbre can tell by the terrified look in his eyes that he is still conscious. The blue woman tugs again and the ropey cords tear out of his body. His mouth is open to scream but only blood comes out. She wraps the sticky ropes around her shoulders, draping them over her like a shawl.

The shark man creeps down the alleyway, sniffing from building to building as a dozen of Dr. Ichii's men fill the corridor. The goons are badly mutated. Timbre doesn't like the crazed looks in their eyes.

"They are hunting for someone," Timbre says to Ohime. "The guy they're looking for must be wounded, the shark can track blood."

Ohime peeks through a crack under the trash can and sees the figure at the end of the alleyway rolling his seaweed cigar between his thumb and index finger. The metal of his suit is turning a pretty green at the seams where it's starting to corrode.

"Let's get out of here" Timbre says to Ohime as she yanks her hand and they sneak away down the alleyway.

***

Ohime tries to pry her hand from Timbre's grasp as she stumbles to keep up with the anemone woman. "Why are you walking so fast?"

In answer, Timbre squeezes Ohime's hand tighter and keeps walking.

"Where are we going next?" Ohime asks.

Timbre stops. She grabs the girl's other hand and pulls her arms so that they are facing each other.

"Do you even know what just happened?" she looks Ohime in the eyes.

"What do you mean?" Ohime says

"The shark? Dr. Ichii and his men?" Timbre looks to see if there is any sign of recognition in the girl's face. She is obviously clueless.

"There was a shark?" Ohime's starfish points perking up.

Timbre can't believe the girl's naïveté. "What's wrong with you? Didn't you see the danger you were in? Dr. Ichii and his men are not people you want to tangle with. They are the most dangerous threat in the dome."

Ohime blinks her violet eyes and then says, "You seem like you need a soak in one of the Concordian hot springs."

"What is wrong with you?"

Ohime shrugs.

"What fucking pod did you hatch out of?"

"Pod-9."

"*What?*"

"Pod-9. That's where my parents raised me."

"What the hell is Pod-9?"

"A bio-research facility on the green water lake. My parents were scientists. I grew up there."

"You've been locked in a lab your whole life?"

"Mostly. I left a few weeks ago, after my parents died. The fire killed everyone but me. All the people were really nice there. Stewart with his talking plants, Sammy with her bubble machine, George and his seashell mandolin. Now I'm looking for more nice people. Like you."

Timbre shakes her head.

"I'm not going to be able to get rid of you, am I?"

"Nope." Ohime smiles.

"You can follow me as far as La Boca."

"Are there more nice people there?"

"I'll make sure you find some nice people. Then you can bug them instead of me."

Before Timbre continues on her path, she looks back into the distance to make sure the gang of mutants aren't following them. The last thing she needs is another run-in with Dr. Ichii.

***

The first time Timbre encountered Dr. Ichii was five years ago. At that time, she was still a teenager living on the streets in Chiba District. She had been on the streets off and on her whole life, even before the collapse. Timbre survived on whatever she could scavenge or steal. She knew that the only person she could trust was herself. She didn't care who she screwed over or took advantage of, as long as she got what she needed to survive.

Abandoned as a child, she became toughened by the harsh living conditions in the slums. She had been beaten, raped, stabbed, robbed, used, abused, molested, degraded, and forced into prostitution repeatedly throughout her childhood until she became as tough as nails. It only made her tougher once the slums filled with crazed mutants.

At first no one knew the cause of the fish mutations. They didn't realize it was the yellow algae that had been spreading across the landscape. Having come in contact with the algae herself, sleeping on it in alleyways or rolling around in it during bar fights, Timbre herself began to change. Her heart felt like a watermelon growing in her chest, stretching apart her ribcage. She lost her hair and the skin on her scalp extended into dreadlocks, then tentacles. As the change happened, a tingling sensation filled her body. Her teeth felt loose in her mouth. Cramps crawled in her stomach. Her mind became foggy and she started getting more and more violent.

At first, she was scared of these changes. She didn't want to lose her mind like the others. Then, once she learned of her ability to paralyze others with her poison darts, she took full advantage of her mutation. It became yet another tool of survival.

Although she was becoming stronger, the streets around her were becoming more dangerous. A government task force was created to analyze the problem of the yellow algae that was contaminating the underwater dome. They discovered that it was the algae that had caused the mutations, and that the more mutated people became the crazier they got. The government issued warnings for everyone to stay inside their homes and they tried to control the algae infestation. But it was a short term solution and soon the algae spread throughout the dome.

Dr. Ichii was a genetic researcher who invented mechanical implants that controlled cell growth and slowed the mutations. He was praised as the savior of the dome, and people flocked to him to get the implants that would preserve their mental stability. Unfortunately, the implants were expensive and complicated to produce, so the prices were unbelievably high. Those who couldn't afford them, including all the poor lower class citizens, mutated more and more until the slums were overrun by murderous fish creatures. Dr. Ichii blamed their leaders for the outbreak of yellow algae and refused to supply them with his implants. The government soon collapsed and only small pockets of humanity survived.

Timbre's survival instinct was strong and she had the necessary skills to protect herself on the streets, but she knew the only way to prevent inevitable insanity was to get her hands on one of Dr. Ichii's implants. She had no money, but that wasn't going to stop her. She knew the only way to survive would be to break into Dr. Ichii's lab and take the implants for herself.

The compound was protected by an army of henchmen, who were armed to the teeth with biomechanical weaponry. There would be no chance she could get through them if she hit them head-on. To get through, Timbre had to crawl up the side of the building, blending in with the red sea flowers that grew along the coral wall. Once inside the compound, she searched each room, looking for the doctor's lab. She moved silently, ducking into the shadows whenever a guard passed, her tentacles coiling like snakes as she crept from doorway to doorway.

There wasn't anyone around when she entered the lab. Her red toes squished against the sterile white ceramic floor as she moved across the room, discovering a wide array of technological devices. Bright blue machines emitted puffs of pink smoke. Vacuum tubes lined the walls, sending green and yellow fluids across the room. Timbre felt as if she had stepped into an alien world.

On a table in the back of the room, she located a stockpile of mechanical parts for the implants. She carefully sorted through the pile, wondering which parts would work for her. Before she could figure out the proper components, she heard a door slam shut. She spun around and locked eyes on barnacle-covered lips as they curled into a smile. It was Dr. Ichii.

"What do you think you're doing?" he bellowed, "What would you have done if you had gotten away with my equipment? Install it yourself?"

Timbre ran toward the door.

"It takes a medical expert with years of experience to perform the necessary surgery for an implant to work," said Dr. Ichii.

Timbre reached the doorway but when she opened it she was charged by a muscular grey shark man. She tried leaping out of the way, swinging her tentacles wildly through the air. The shark man ducked her whips of hair and Timbre could see a circular saw spinning on his back below her. The shark reached out and grabbed Timbre by the leg and she dropped, hitting her head on the table on the way down to the floor. The mechanical parts were knocked off the table, scattering all around her. The shark man pressed his booted heel into the center of her chest, pinning her down. Dr. Ichii laughed again and came over to stare down into her face.

"I'm impressed you were able to make it this far into my compound," he said, "Not just anybody could get past my defenses. It takes a lot of skill, and audacity."

Timbre struggled underneath the weight of the shark man. She tried releasing her poison darts, but his knee was on her tentacle hair, the weight shooting pains through her head. One tentacle felt like it was going to split open.

"Tell you what," Dr. Ichii continued, "I'll cut you a deal. You work for me and I'll give you the implant."

Timbre stared up at him, her red eyes piercing straight into his without blinking. When shark man ground his knee down harder against her tentacles, she didn't flinch. Instead, she smiled.

"I'll take that as a yes," said Ichii.

CHAPTER FOUR

Ohime kicks a seashell down the path in front of her, chases after it and kicks it again. Timbre walks slowly behind her, the heels of her stilettos clicking like a metronome set on adagio. Ohime's seashell skitters across the road and falls into the river. She runs over to the silver water and peers down into it to look for the shell. A colony of hermit crabs dance below the surface. Each crab is unique: one crab has a shell made out of a bottle cap, another has made a shell out of the claw of a much larger crab, a third crab's shell looks like a baby's ear and another shell looks like an eyeball that peers up at Ohime and blinks.

"See those buildings up ahead," says Timbre, pointing in front of her, "that's La Boca. That's where we will part ways."

Ohime abandons her search for the seashell and looks in the direction Timbre is pointing. Ohime thinks La Boca looks beautiful. The buildings are constructed from boxes and crates piled on top of each other. All are brightly painted different colors, creating a mismatched rainbow town that looks like it could topple over at any moment.

"What a dump," says Timbre, "It's like these people have carved buildings out of trash."

Ohime notices a mural of a couple dancing tango painted on the side of one of the buildings.

"It's lovely here," says Ohime.

They come to a doorway of a shop with an open sign above it and walk in. The shop is dimly lit with a long counter and shelves containing all sorts of gadgets, radio valves, pipes, pressure gauges, assorted plumbing and gears. The only other person in the shop is a tall barracuda woman in long Victorian style dress with a high collar and a large hat.

Timbre and Ohime walk around the shop browsing a row of hydro-bicycles leaning against the wall in the corner. A man emerges from a doorway behind the counter.

"Oh hello," the man says, smiling. "I didn't hear you come in."

He spins around to the front of the counter and bows to them. Ohime bows her head back in acknowledgement. He is a head shorter than Ohime and has wheels instead of legs.

Ohime imagines what it would be like to have wheels for legs. She looks down at her shoes and then hears the man say, "You look like you could use some cheering up."

He hands Ohime a big pink lollipop shaped like a seashell.

She accepts it and smiles, "Thank you!"

She puts the lollipop in her mouth, "So sweet."

The man does a little jig, hoping from side to side bouncing on each wheel. Ohime thinks it's cute and giggles at him while sucking on the lollipop.

Timbre fidgets with the knobs on a recumbent bike. She checks the two steam pipes on the sides of the back wheel, then adjusts the tension on the gears with the tip of her red finger.

"Do any of these bikes work?" Timbre asks the shopkeeper.

"Well, none of them are very pretty," he says, whirring over to her, "but with a little patience, they'll get you where you need to go. We've got to make the best of what we've got, you know what I mean?"

Timbre nods at him and squeezes a handful of spokes in one tire that is slightly bent.

"That one needs a new derailleur," he says

Timbre adjusts one of the spoke nipples and spins the wheel. The man looks up at her and says, "How far do you need to go?"

"Ghoshi Territory," Timbre replies.

"Well, you'll be needing a better bike than that to go through the wasteland," he says, "I've been tinkering with something in the back. It looks like you know bikes. Maybe you'd like to come back and a take a look at it."

Timbre nods and follows him as he whirrs back behind the counter. She looks over her shoulder at Ohime, who is admiring a collection of glass bottles on a shelf by the door.

Ohime picks up one of the glass bottles and shakes it. Inside, a tornado of glitter swirls around the clear blue liquid. She wonders what the liquid is and places it back on the shelf. She looks around the shop for Timbre who isn't visible from the back room. When she turns back around, the barracuda woman is standing right in front of her. The center of the woman's dress has been cut away to reveal a glass belly like a fish bowl. Around the edges of the implant is a shiny brass ring.

The woman flashes her long teeth and stares into Ohime's eyes as she says, "Are you new in town?"

Ohime takes a step backward and nods.

"I haven't seen a starfish quite so lovely as you," the barracuda woman says. She reaches out and adjusts one of the purple bows on Ohime's dress.

"What a beautiful outfit." The barracuda blinks her long eyelashes and the edges of her mouth curl up, creating deep creases in the sides of her scaly face.

"Thank you," Ohime fidgets with the same purple bow on her dress, readjusting to the way it was before, and takes another step back from the woman.

"You have such beautiful features," says the barracuda. Then she strokes one of Ohime's starfish points and curls one of her fingers around the end of it. "Beautiful violet eyes."

Ohime blushes and looks away from the woman. She sucks on her lollipop. She wonders where Timbre went.

"Is that woman your mother?" asks the barracuda.

The barracuda woman tilts her pointed chin to the side. The ribbon on her maroon hat flops while she walks closer to Ohime, cornering her against the row of bikes.

"No," says Ohime, a bicycle handlebar jabbing into her hip.

"Your sister?"

"No, I just met her today."

Ohime looks down at the woman's fishbowl belly. She can see her stomach contents through the glass. They appear to be small fish bones, digesting in her visible stomach acids.

"Do your parents know that you're with such a strange woman?" As the woman leans in closer, the bones in her glass belly jangle around like charms on a bracelet.

"No, my parents are dead," says Ohime.

"Oh you poor, pretty, thing," says the woman, her fishy breath hot against Ohime's eyelids. "It must be devastating to lose your parents at such a young age. I couldn't imagine. And to be stuck with that lowlife scum of a—"

The woman is interrupted by the sound of Timbre's metal stiletto tapping on the floor, as she comes out from behind the counter with a hydro-bike. The bike is shiny with brass gears and two large steam pipes flanking each wheel. A gold tuba-shaped engine sits behind the metal hub of the triangular frame. The wheels, designed for off-roading, click-click against the stone floor as the bike is wheeled through the store.

The barracuda woman returns to browsing the shelves as Ohime runs over to Timbre. She runs so fast that she doesn't realize the shopkeeper rolling in front of her and she slams into him. He wobbles a bit on his wheels from the force of her impact, but instead of getting upset he chuckles a deep belly laugh.

"Sorry," Ohime says, but the shop keeper has already forgotten about it.

"How's that lollipop my dear?" he asks Ohime.

She pulls the stick from her mouth and the shell is now just a shard of pink. She smiles brightly, "Delicious, thank you."

"I'm leaving you here," Timbre tells Ohime. "Samuel says he'll look after you and give you a place to stay as long as you help out in the shop."

Samuel gives her a big smile. "How does that sound,

kiddo? Would you mind helping out an old cripple like me?"

Ohime looks at the two of them. Samuel seems nice enough, but she would rather be with Timbre.

"Why are you going?" Ohime asks Timbre.

"The wasteland is no place for a girl like you my dear," Samuel says. "My wife and I are so thrilled to have another pair of hands around here. Ever since our daughter died, we've—"

Timbre cuts him off. "I don't need you slowing me down, kid. I told you, when we got to La Boca we're parting ways."

"But…" Ohime says, but before she can finish her thought Timbre cranks the knob on the side of the bike and with a loud roar of the bubbling engine she rides away, leaving a cloud of dust that swirls into Ohime's petticoats.

Samuel looks down at Ohime and pats her puffy-sleeved shoulder. "Don't feel so bad, kiddo. I'm sure you'll see her again someday."

"But she was so nice," Ohime says. "Exactly the kind of person I was looking for . . ."

Ohime's eyes droop down to her feet. Samuel can tell she needs a moment to herself.

"Wait here," Samuel says to Ohime, "I'm going to go tell my wife to get your room ready for you." He clasps his hands together under his chin and wobble-spins out the back door.

Ohime stands in the doorway, confused about what to do next. She is used to being on her own, but she isn't sure why Timbre just left her like that. She turns around and the barracuda woman is right in front of her again.

"What's wrong dear?" says the Barracuda woman. "Did that soulless bitch abandon you?"

"Timbre is a nice person," Ohime says. "She saved my life. She—"

The woman waves her words away and says, "Whatever will you do now? Have you a place to stay?"

"Yeah . . .um, Samuel and his wife—"

"Oh dear, don't tell me that you're being taken in by that dirty old man? That would be ghastly!" The woman leans in so close that Ohime can see silvery fish scales stuck between her jagged barracuda teeth. "You know he's a complete pervert, right? He has a thing for young girls. All he wants from you is to be his personal live-in whore. He wants to see your pretty little lips around his wrinkled old cock."

Ohime's eyes widen. She can't believe what this woman is telling her. She looks around to see if Samuel is anywhere nearby, but he is nowhere to be seen.

"Trust me, my dear. A pretty thing like you should not let that monster anywhere near you."

"But, what am I going to do?" asks Ohime. "He seemed like a nice person."

"You can come stay with me. I have a big house with lots of rooms."

Ohime looks at the woman and blinks the long lashes framing her violet eyes. "Are you a nice person?"

"Of course I am! And I know lots of nice people I could introduce you to." The woman holds out her hand for Ohime to shake. "My name is Sphyraena, everyone calls me Miss Rae."

Miss Rae smiles when she takes her hand.

"I'm Ohime."

After they shake, the woman doesn't let go of her hand.

"Come on sweetheart. Miss Rae will take good care of you."

***

Miss Rae and Ohime enter the woman's large rose-colored seashell house. It's more like a palace than a house. Several tall buildings arranged in a square with a large garden courtyard in the center. The walls are heavily ornamented with rocks and shells. Everything is shiny pink with pearls and opalescent sea forms. In the center of the courtyard is a large statue of a voluptuous woman carved out of bone. She is standing in a giant oyster shell. Around her feet are placed offerings of seaweed fruit and flower petals. The air is perfumed with the smell of fresh flowers. Miss Rae invites Ohime to sit at one of the tables in the courtyard. She rings a little bell and a girl dressed in a gauzy robe brings in a delicate moon shell tea pot and a plate of brightly colored sushi.

"Since you are a starfish, is it true that you can extend your stomach from your body to eat?" Miss Rae asks.

"No." Ohime giggles and reaches out for a piece of sushi. It has been hours since she's had anything to eat.

The flavor lights up her taste buds when she takes her first bite. Ohime smiles at Miss Rae as she chews, grateful for the woman's hospitality. At first she thought Miss Rae was rather strange, but now she thinks the woman might be very nice. Ohime examines the woman's outfit and notices how beautiful her dress is. She likes the embroidered circlet of starfish lining the brass ring around her fishbowl belly. She admires the lace cuffs on the sleeves of the wine-colored dress.

After they finish their tea, Miss Rae asks Ohime if she needs anything else.

"Actually, um, I am a bit embarrassed to ask."

The woman's scaly eyebrows go up.

"Do you have any sponges?" she whispers.

Miss Rae smiles, showing her sharp teeth. "On your moon eh? Of course, you dear thing. I will be right back"

Miss Rae leaves and when she returns she hands Ohime two pink sea sponges. Ohime thinks they are almost as nice as the ones she collected this morning. She puts them into her crabshell purse for later.

Miss Rae invites Ohime to have a rest in one of the rooms surrounding the courtyard. She takes her into one that is decorated with red velvet drapes and mirrors on the ceiling. Ohime is fascinated by all of the detail put into the decoration of the room and turns to thank Miss Rae, but the barracuda woman is already gone.

Having the whole room to herself, Ohime looks up and twirls around in circles, admiring herself in the mirrored ceiling. It's fun for her to see the way her dress parasols out and the starfish points on her head stand straight up—she can even see the shiny pink dots at their tips. Mid-spin, she stops when she sees a large man with hideous fish mutations entering the room. He is nearly twice her size, his chestnut skin is covered in puss-filled polyps that are red and swollen and he smells oily and rotten. Ohime isn't sure why he is here. She curls her mouth into a half smile.

"That's a pretty dress," says the man.

"Thanks!" Ohime's smile widens.

The fish man walks toward her, taking slow laborious

steps. He is breathing heavily. His nostrils flare.

"You smell so . . . ripe" he says.

Ohime takes a step back toward the corner of the room. She is getting a weird feeling about this guy. She's not sure what he wants but he has a look in his eye that makes her feel really uncomfortable.

"Don't worry, I'm not going to hurt you," he says, "I just want to taste you." He licks his thick gummy lips with his long fish tongue.

He backs her against the velvety wall and places his large webbed hands on the wall on each side of her shoulders. "You are so beautiful"

"Um, I really should go find Miss Rae," Ohime says. "I forgot to ask her for something." She ducks underneath his arms and hurries toward the door, her rocking horse shoes clattering on the seashell flooring.

"You're not going anywhere," he says and grabs her by the waist. She lets out a high-pitched scream and struggles to get away. The fish man pins her arms with one of his webbed hands. He lifts her into the air and tosses her over his shoulder; her skirt flies up and covers part of his face. He blows it out of his eyes with a big puff of air from his thick gummy lips. She kicks her feet around wildly until she plants one of her heels into his eye.

"You bitch!" he screams, covering his face.

Ohime wriggles free of his grasp and runs out of the room. Her heart clatters in her chest. The points on her starfish bend back in a panic. The fish man follows after her, still holding his eye. She can see red beginning to ooze from below his hands. Darting madly through the courtyard, she searches the rooms for Miss Rae. She opens a random door and inside the room sees a colorful carp woman sucking on a man's toes. He rubs his fist along his exposed penis, moaning. Every other part of him is covered in metal scales. The carp woman is naked, exposing the colorful patterns adoring her entire body; natural tattoos. Both people stop what they are doing and look at Ohime like something is wrong with her.

Ohime's eyes widen and she slams shut the door. She continues running down the breezeway and up a staircase, her black pigtails swing back and forth behind her. She looks back and sees the blinded fish man lumbering up the stairs, wheezing and coughing. She hurries up to another door and pulls it open.

Inside there are two wrasse people with brightly colored heads. The thick lips of the male wrasse latch onto the other's vaginal lips, sucking on a gooey bluish liquid coating her skin.

Her breathing gets faster and faster until she convulses. Her eyes roll back in her head and she arches her spine so Ohime can see between her legs; her vaginal opening is transforming itself.

A shiny blue and pink-swirled protrusion grows until it is shaped like a penis. The woman's breasts shrink until she looks like a man. She grins her wide protractile mouth, showing off her teeth and then she forces her penis deep into the male's throat. She has him suck on her new appendage until he gags. Then she flips the male fish over and thrusts her new penis into his anus. She moans, reaching around his waist to jerk him off as she fucks him.

Ohime closes the door, turns and runs all the way down the hall to a room in the corner of the courtyard. The quality of the light is different here, softer. The air is more heavily perfumed.

She peeks in the room and sees Miss Rae masturbating with a small fish man. He is about five inches long. He has the torso, arms and head of a human, but his lower half is a fish tail. His scales are silver. She holds him between her breasts, and moans as he sucks her nipples. His fish tail slaps the underside of her breast. She grins down at him and he looks up at her fearfully, his tiny fish mouth tightly suctioning around her nipple. She pries him from her nipple and slides his silvery body down her skin past her round glass belly and holds him close to her. Then she slides him face first toward her vaginal opening.

He struggles, reaching out his arms and grabbing onto her vulva, pulling her pubic hair to prevent himself from being shoved all the way inside. But she pushes more insistently until only the end of his tail is still sticking out. It flaps wildly back and forth and she moans in pleasure as it smacks against her clitoris. Then she swiftly pulls him out. He's gasping for breath and she kisses him. She licks his face. She sucks her juices off of his small body. He is fresh and salty. His tiny fish penis becomes erect as she licks the length of his small body. She sucks on his scales and then she slurps him into her mouth.

She can feel him struggling to climb back up her throat as she swallows him. Her orgasm rises like a coiled snake through her spine. She closes her eyes and tilts her head back in pleasure as he slides the rest of the way down to her belly. She then looks down and through her glass abdomen she sees his fish body thrashing wildly about as he is being digested. The movement inside her excites her more and she screams out in climax as he swims around terrified within her round fish tank belly.

Ohime can see the man's terrified face inside Miss

Rae's stomach. She's not sure what to think. She feels a strange sensation in her stomach like moths hitting glass, she hears bees buzzing in her ears. Then suddenly a hand clamps over her mouth and she is yanked backward by the pustule-riddled fish man.

Ohime kicks her legs out in front of her and knocks over a large conch shell urn. The sound of it breaking against the floor alarms Miss Rae who comes out into the hallway, wrapped in a silk kimono. The kimono only half-covers her belly, so Ohime can still see the terrified face of the man swimming inside her as the stomach acids begin to eat away at his skin.

"What's going on out here?" she asks, "why aren't you in your room?"

The fish man says, "This little whore fucking blinded me! And I paid double because she was menstruating!" He grabs the barracuda woman by her throat and pushes her up against the pink coral wall. "Give me my money back, and another girl for free, or I'll—"

Miss Rae croaks out, "Yes, of course, choose anyone you'd like, on the house."

The fish man releases Miss Rae and she coddles him. "You poor thing, let me take a look at your eye." He removes his hand and Miss Rae makes hushing noises and pats him on the shoulder. She rings a bell and another girl in a gauzy robe pokes out of a nearby shadow. She tells the girl, "Please take Mr. Maraschino to the lounge and help him clean up. Then make sure that he is well taken care of." The girl bows, then helps the fish man amble down the hallway, kissing his eyelid with her thin eel tongue, to make it all better.

After he leaves, Miss Rae turns to Ohime, "You good

for nothing piece of shit, he's one of my best customers. I am not going to have a little cunt like you ruining my business. You're going to be punished for this."

Miss Rae drags Ohime by her pigtails back to the red velvet room. Ohime doesn't understand what is happening. She doesn't understand why Miss Rae locks her in the room and leaves her there.

Then Ohime hears a loud crash. She looks out the window of the room and sees a swarm of jellyfish women descending from the sky above the courtyard. They parachute in, drifting slowly to the ground, their long tentacles like hair that reaches all the way past their ankles. They are wearing harajuku makeup, bright pink jackets and white tutu skirts and wide belts, knee socks and colorful boots.

Ohime thinks they are beautiful and graceful but she also sees the same crazed look in their eyes as the crabmen who attacked her earlier. She knows that they must have spent too much time in the yellow algae. One of the jellyfish women snatches up a fish whore and then wraps her tentacle hair around the woman stinging her until she goes limp. More of the jellyfish women start opening doors and attacking the occupants within. Ohime sees Miss Rae across the courtyard, she swings her fists at a jellyfish. The pink jelly woman slams her rainbow boot into Miss Rae's glass implant and shatters it. Miss Rae lets out a painful shriek as liquid bursts out and the fish man flops around on the floor, screaming in pain from the stomach acid still coating him.

Ohime knows she has to get out of here. She searches the room and decides to throw a red velvet footstool through the window. The glass sprays everywhere and Ohime steps carefully out through the broken window into the courtyard. She quickly makes her way along the walls, trying not to attract too much attention to herself and runs down the steps out into the street.

***

Timbre is on her hydro-bike just outside of La Boca. She glances back over her shoulder and notices a swarm of crazed jellyfish descending upon the town.

What in the hell? she thinks.

She turns the bike around.

The streets are filled with jellyfish people descending from the sky. They drift gently down like bubbles. Timbre whips her head around while she drives down the narrow street, her tentacles slicing through the jellyfish, their rubbery torsos popping like balloons. Timbre releases her poison darts and five jellyfish girls drop to the ground paralyzed. Their transparent tentacles squish beneath the tires of Timbre's bike as she rides over them on her way back to the shop.

Outside the shop, lying in the street, she sees Samuel. She rides over to him as he lays upturned on the ground, his wheels spinning in the air. She jumps off her bike and bends down to him and says, "Where is Ohime?"

Samuel's eyes tear up and before he can explain, the jellyfish poison overcomes him. His body twists in pain on the ground as he takes his last breath.

Ohime rushes out of the brothel as screaming fish whores are scooped up into the jellyfish tentacles. She runs down the street and sees Timbre up ahead flinging poison darts at the descending jellyfish women around her. They fly back, away from her attacks, and then float slowly toward her when her back is turned.

The girl runs into Timbre's arms and holds her tightly. The starfish on the top of her head glowing a deep purple.

"I knew you'd come back for me!" Ohime cries.

"Yeah, yeah," Timbre says, pushing her away.

Then they get on her bike and ride off, cutting down the jellyfish floating into their path.

CHAPTER FIVE

The giant bioluminescent sea mushrooms cluster into a forest around Timbre as she rides the hydro-bike through the tall green stalks that stretch up into the sky. The large glowing green mushroom caps almost touch the top of the glass dome. Ohime's face is tickled by Timbre's chili-pepper tentacles as she leans her head against the woman's back, hugging her tightly, sitting snugly behind her on the bike seat. Timbre is trying to avoid driving over any seaweed pods. The pods are filled with greasy orange liquid that makes the tires slippery against the road.

Using only one hand to steer, Timbre reaches for the dome map. She carefully navigates through the cumbersome vegetation while checking her map in the green glow of the mushroom canopies. The terrain has become extremely overgrown. Her map tells her this is a highway, but what she sees before her is barely a path. It doesn't look like anyone uses these roads anymore. The mushrooms have taken over. Seashell pavement crumbles under her tires, damaged from the fungi. The whole area smells like rotting meat.

At one time, the dome was a thriving underwater

country with its own economy. It was the first and last of its kind, built as a contained ecosystem to allow people to live underwater because of overpopulation. But as life on the surface became uninhabitable, it was the only place left on earth not affected by the pollution, disease, famine, and war that eventually wiped out most of the population on land. The underwater dome became the only place where people could live. Space was limited, and only skilled laborers and those that could afford the high price of admission survived. Those few survivors soon became the last, as all life on the surface died out. Over time, the civilization inside the biodome evolved. Five generations of people living in the dome have never seen land or sky. It is well known that life is not sustainable on the polluted surface of the planet. But ever since the yellow algae, life down here is dying out as well. Only the tough will survive.

The way Ohime's breath feels on her back, Timbre can tell that the girl has fallen asleep. It surprises Timbre how trusting and relaxed this girl is. She is still so innocent. Timbre was a lot different when she was Ohime's age. She had already learned that it was better not to get attached to anyone. She knew how to take care of herself and she grew up fast, especially after she started working for Dr. Ichii.

Dr. Ichii had many enemies. He took in orphans and street criminals and trained them to protect him in exchange for the implants that would prevent them from going crazy. Not only did they guard Dr. Ichii from the crazed fish mutants skulking through the slummy neighborhood outside of his compound, they also shut down the operations of any rival scientists who might get in his way of dominating the implant development field. Ichii's henchmen were very loyal to him and Timbre was no exception. Timbre was a good fighter even before meeting the scientist, having survived out in the streets for so long, but with Ichii's training she became his top assassin.

Out of all of Ichii's henchmen, Timbre was the quickest and most deadly. There seemed to be more than just a passion for survival behind her eyes. Each time she fought, her body became an instrument of death. No longer a woman or a sea anemone, she was her own type of weapon. It was as if all of the hate and torture she had absorbed in her abusive life was being channeled back out of her with deadly force.

She could summersault through the air, whips of hair chopping down her enemies on all sides and land perfectly still in the middle of a garden of sea flowers without disturbing any of them. She was adept at deception and espionage. At Ichii's instruction she would sneak into rival research facilities and set them on fire. She would seduce and assassinate anyone with power who wouldn't submit to Dr. Ichii's influence. With lightning speed she could use her tentacle hair to sever arms and legs, and with a tilt of her head she could release dozens of paralyzing darts. It was not unusual for her to single-handedly kill off a group of crazed mutants without breaking a sweat.

But her job wasn't always about killing people. On one particular occasion Ichii ordered Timbre on a mission to hold a young girl hostage to extort technology from her parents who did research for Pod-2. Timbre didn't like being stuck with the stupid task of babysitting so she locked the girl in the closet and used the kid's pet lobster-dog as target practice.

"Chill the fuck out, Timbre," said Igo, the lanky red-skinned eel man.

Timbre flipped him off.

Igo leaned against the kitchen counter, eating a seaweed donut through rubbery black lips, as Timbre threw darts at the whining lobster-dog tied to a rotating ceiling fan.

"You know, you need to learn how to relax," said Igo with crumbs on his baggy chin. "These slow missions are the only chance we get to sit back and enjoy ourselves."

Timbre put a dart right through the dog's lobster face and turned to her partner. "I fucking hate these kinds of missions. They're a waste of my abilities."

Igo licked his lips and walked over to the woman.

"You're always so tense." He stepped around behind her and rubbed a finger down one of her anemone tentacles. "That is, except when you're killing people."

She turned to face him, uncomfortable with anyone getting behind her.

"I know something else that could relieve that tension," Igo said, caressing her tentacle more firmly. "Let me show you." He glared at her, sticking his long fishy tongue out of his mouth, coiling it slowly around his right nipple.

"How many times do I have to tell you?" Timbre said. She whipped her tentacles away from his fingers, decapitating the dead lobster-dog and its body fell from the ceiling fan. "You try to fuck me and I'll kill you."

Igo stepped away from her and laughed at her outburst. "I'm going to fuck you someday. You just wait and see."

"And on that day you are going to die," she said.

The front door burst open and a young blue-skinned girl with a rooster fish mohawk entered. Timbre shoved

Igo out of her way with her shoulder and approached the girl.

"It's about time, Freya." She angrily shook her head, as if it were the girl's fault she had to wait so long. "How'd it go?"

"The scientist complied," Freya said with a monotone voice. "We need to bring the girl to the rendezvous point in fifteen minutes."

Timbre nodded. "Let's go."

***

The little guppy girl was curled in a ball crying into her knees when Timbre opened the closet door.

"Come out," Timbre said, pointing at the floor.

The little girl looked over Timbre's shoulder and saw her dog's severed head rotating on the ceiling fan. She screamed and backed into a corner, covering her eyes from the morbid sight.

Timbre groaned and said, "I don't have time for this shit."

She grabbed the kid by the hair and ripped her out of the closet. The child screamed and tried to push Timbre's red hands out of her grip as she was dragged through the living room.

"You don't have to be so mean to her," Igo said. "She's just a kid."

"I fucking hate kids," she said on the way out of the door.

***

The kid's fish-headed father didn't come alone. He was accompanied by two large sea bass bodyguards who stood twenty yards behind him. Freya and Igo stayed twenty yards behind Timbre as she took the girl toward her father. Timbre kept a firm grip around the back of the little girl's neck. She was still crying, rubbing a bald patch on her scalp where her hair had been ripped out.

"Where is it?" Timbre asked the father.

The man was calm. His bug-eyed fish head stuck out of a nicely pressed black business suit. He was the most presentable man Timbre had seen in years. His two bodyguards were also in nice suits. They were a stark contrast to all the debris and yellow algae in the streets around them. He held up a briefcase.

"How could you work for a monster like Dr. Ichii?" he asked Timbre.

She didn't have the patience for talk. "Just hand it over."

"He's a cruel, selfish megalomaniac who will be the death of what is left of our society."

"Watch your words," Timbre said, gripping his child's neck tighter until the girl cried out.

The father acknowledged his daughter's pain, but continued his speech. "Do you even know what those implants are doing to you?"

"My patience is wearing thin," Timbre said. "You have one more second to give me that briefcase or I'm killing you and your kid."

The fish-headed man frowned at her. "Fine, go ahead and die as one of Ichii's dogs."

Then he tossed the briefcase over and Timbre caught it with her free hand. She let go of the kid and examined the contents of the within the case. It was all there, exactly as Dr. Ichii described. The guppy girl ran to her father and he knelt down to greet her, patting her forehead.

"Are you okay, my love?" he asked his daughter.

The girl could hardly speak through her tears. "The mean lady killed Claw and pulled my hair out."

The scientist brushed the girl's hair out of her crying fish eyes. "Don't worry, sweetheart. She won't hurt you anymore."

Timbre turned around and walked toward her associates with the goods.

"I hate her," the girl said.

"Of course you do," said the father, hugging her tightly. "She's an evil piece of trash."

Timbre stopped in her tracks. She turned around and raced at the scientist. The little girl didn't realize that her father had been decapitated until the blood rained down on the top of her head. She looked up to see a fountain of blood coming out of the collar of his business suit. The little girl was in too much shock to scream.

The two bodyguards didn't have time to react as a volley of poison darts hit them in their chests. Timbre didn't even have to look at the guards when she killed them, staring down on the little guppy girl still embracing her headless father.

The little girl looked up at her with her mouth hanging open. Her bulbous tearing fish eyes asked one question: *why?*

"He was right," Timbre told the girl. "I am an evil piece of trash."

She left the girl in her father's blood and walked over to her associates.

"You didn't need to kill him," Igo told her as she handed him the briefcase.

Timbre shrugged as she walked past.

CHAPTER SIX

For several days, Ohime and Timbre have been traveling through Ghoshi Territory. Ohime lost the heel of her rocking horse shoe in the honeycomb coral hills. Their bike broke down while passing through the underwater lava fields. Ohime dropped their map into a nest of giant red sea spiders hidden in a field of blue algae. By the time they made it over the cephalopod mountains they had run out of food.

Tired, sore, and hungry they finally arrive at a place where they can get a hot meal and a warm bed. All they have to do is cross the pink swamp stretching in the distance before them. Timbre explains to Ohime that the only person she knows in Ghoshi Territory lives on an island in the middle of this swamp. He'll surely take them in for the night and hopefully give them some food and supplies to take with them for the rest of their journey.

The color of the swamp makes Timbre's stomach turn as she looks down at it.

"Stay out of the pink goo," Timbre says, "If you fall in, this stuff will suck you under so fast I wouldn't be able to save you."

Ohime leans over and looks at the swirl pink liquid and slips on her heelless shoe. Timbre grabs her in the nick of time.

"What did I just tell you?"

"But I like pink . . ."

Ohime sees a big blue rock moving slowly toward her in the distance. At first she is afraid, but as the pink goop drips off the top of the rock, Ohime can see the large mellow eyes of the creature.

"Bog turtles," Timbre says.

The turtle looks up at them with big glossy eyes.

"So cute!" Ohime says to the turtle.

"We can ride them across to the island," Timbre tells Ohime as another one of the blue turtles swims up to her. It's chewing on a piece of sea grass and blinks its long green eyelashes slowly at her. Ohime examines the slimy back of the turtle more closely. Tiny purple spirals decorate the blue shell. She reaches out and traces one of them with her finger. The turtle blows a puff of air out of its huge nostrils, the force of its breath fluttering the ribbons in Ohime's hair.

Timbre jumps atop of a turtle in one fluid motion, its shell is so big her legs don't even come close to touching the pink goo. She grabs onto the turtle's ears and yanks backward. The creature lurches forward with a splash as Timbre confidently rides its back. Ohime takes a step back from the edge of the bog.

"Come on, get on that turtle," Timbre points at the creature nearest Ohime.

Ohime stares back at her blankly.

"You pull back on the ears to steer them," Timbre says.

Ohime worries that she won't be able to handle a turtle by herself but before she can say anything, Timbre's turtle sets off swimming in the direction of the island.

Ohime gently pets the spirals on the shell of the turtle. She whispers hello to it and then quietly crawls onto its back, carefully adjusting her petticoats as she perches in the center of the shell. She reaches out and strokes the turtle on the top of its head and gently starts to take one of its ears in her palm. But just as she clasps one ear, the turtle turns its head the other direction, causing the creature to jolt forward with a scream of pain. Ohime lets go of the ear and hugs onto the turtle's neck, trying not to fall into the pink gooey sludge. Timbre looks back at her and sees the turtle is beginning to descend into the fluid.

"Grab the ears!" she screams at Ohime.

"I don't want to hurt it," Ohime says, as the turtle dives deeper.

Timbre groans and rides her turtle toward the girl's. She leans down alongside of the turtle shell and dips her arm into the soup to pull the creature's head out of the liquid. She shoves its head into Ohime's direction.

Ohime takes the ears of the turtle gently into her hands and strokes them softly. Timbre continues on. The creature swims around in circles a few times and then starts munching again on some seaweed. Ohime hears a clicking sound in the grass outside the swamp. Her heart starts beating faster and she knows she needs to catch up with Timbre.

She closes her eyes tight and with the tiniest tug on the ears the turtle stops chewing the seaweed and begins to swim out toward the island in the center of the swamp.

Ohime looks down into the pink goo and sees what

looks like ghosts, faces of fish, and mermaids. The pink water sparkles and glitters. It rolls off the broad fins of the turtle as it gently glides across the goo.

In the distance, Ohime sees a broken down factory. It takes up almost the entirety of the small island. There are towering smoke stacks covered in seaweed vines and a giant warehouse crumbling into ruin. The sides of the building are covered in green furry slime. A small section on one side looks like it has been constructed out of recycled machinery.

When they reach land, the turtles climb up onto the beach to eat shrubbery growing from the side of the building. Timbre slides off of the shell of her turtle and takes a look around. Ohime holds out her hands so the woman can help her down, but Timbre doesn't pay attention to her. Ohime gets down from the shell herself, plopping butt-first onto the ground. Then she gets to her feet and tries to rub the pink goo off of her dress with a stick.

The two of them search the property. The windows are clockwork gears with stained glass inserted into them. There is a network of pneumatic tubes connecting various rooms to one another big enough for a small person to fit into. A row of smashed up video screens line one hallway and all of the lights are out inside the building.

As they explore, Ohime discovers her favorite part of the island is the statuary. There are stone fish with butterfly wings hanging like gargoyles above the doorways and a mermaid fountain in the entryway. Timbre climbs up the crumbling stairs of the mechanical section and calls out "Cedric! Hey Cedric! Where are you?"

After searching the entire property, Timbre determines

that her friend is long gone. It doesn't look like anyone has lived here for a while. *He was an old man*, she thought. *He might be dead by now.*

One good thing comes out of their search, which is that they discover a pantry fully stocked with food. After their long journey, Timbre and Ohime gorge themselves on canned dragon fruit cocktail and sea cucumber stew. They decide to spend the night.

***

While Ohime sleeps, Timbre thinks about her friend Cedric. Timbre never had any friends until she met Cedric. Cedric the blowfish man was one of Dr. Ichii's engineers; he worked in the lab constructing the implants. He was the only nice guy in the place. It was an odd relationship because he was the most open, optimistic, fun-loving person around and she was cold, ruthless and never cared about anyone but herself.

They became friends when she discovered he played chess. Growing up on the streets she used to play fairy chess with old men in the park. She liked it because it taught her strategy and tactics she considered important for survival. She wanted to maintain those skills while working for Dr. Ichii but had no one to play with until Cedric.

At first when they played together, she never spoke but he would talk throughout the entire game.

"Human life is precious," Cedric said. "You should take better care of yourself and have more respect for the people around you."

Timbre looked down at the hexagonal chess board, the mother of pearl surface was iridescent. The pieces, carefully handcrafted by Cedric, were brass clockwork fish. She ignored his banter, winding the key on the side of her octopus and watched it move three cells. Eight tiny little sucker feet gripping the board as its mechanical body captured Cedric's knight. She snickered.

"The implants allow us to withstand the effects of the algae, but what kind of life are we preserving if we are killing each other to make it happen?" Cedric asked his bishop as he wound its key in response to Timbre's move.

Timbre glared at him and calculated her next attack. Cedric smiled back at her. He twisted some gears on the implant in his chest and groaned slightly.

"This old clockwork heart's going to give out on me one of these days," he chuckled.

She studied the board more closely and realized that he had bested her again. She stood up, her frustrated tentacles knocking over all of the pieces on the board as she turned her head and quickly left the room.

Cedric always won. But every week she came back to play. She would show up at his lab each Thursday evening and he would greet her with a big smile. At first she never liked that smile, but eventually she came to consider it comforting, perhaps even the happiest moment of her week. Timbre was determined to win, and she refused to give up until she beat him.

Eventually, Timbre started opening up to Cedric because she realized that it was a good strategy. After listening to Cedric blabber on and on during their games for weeks she understood that he employed this babble as a distraction and she intended to use it against him.

"It's a cruel world," Timbre said, "and taking what you need is essential to survival."

She eyed the pile of fish pawns she had already captured squirming by the edge of the chess board. Some of the clockwork inside them was still ticking, making them look like fish out of water, struggling to breathe air.

"If we are going to survive," said Cedric, "we have to learn to work together and help each other."

"You're wrong," Timbre said, "it's weak to rely on others."

Cedric looked down at the board. "There's an old saying," he said as he wound the key on his next piece, "When the chess game is over, the pawn and the king go back to the same box." He set his piece on the board and watched it capture Ohime's queen. "No one person is better than another and we all need each other."

Timbre lost another game.

Even though they were opposites, they became good friends. She continued playing him, getting a little closer to beating him each time. She knew it wouldn't be long until she had a victory.

One day when she arrived at his lab he didn't have a smile on his face. They started their game in silence and played for a good hour without saying a single word to each other. After he lost both knights, two pieces he rarely ever gave up, Cedric looked at her and said "I have something very important to tell you." His face took a grim shape. "And you have to promise to listen to me."

Timbre looked at him quizzically; usually he was never this serious.

"I've discovered that the upgrades that Dr. Ichii has made to the implants do more than just slow the fish mutations." Cedric looked Timbre in the eyes, "He's using the implants to control people's minds."

Timbre wasn't sure how to respond. She was starting to think that maybe Cedric had cracked. She studied the chess board.

"I am leaving," he said. "I have to get away from this and I want you to come with me."

"What are you talking about old man?" Timbre asked.

"Ichii is insane. He has taken control of people's minds. If you continue working for him you will lose your free will."

"I think you are the one starting to go crazy," she said, "and if you are trying to distract me, it's not going to work."

"I am dead serious," he said, "Don't trust him. We need to leave. Ichii is going to destroy all civilization."

"You are starting to piss me off," Timbre said. "You had better watch what you say about Dr. Ichii. He is the only reason that we are still alive. I would still be on the streets right now if not for him."

Cedric stopped winding the key on his clockwork frog, stood up and said, "Have it your way, but don't say I didn't warn you." Then he turned away and left the room.

Timbre looked down at the chess board and noticed that Cedric left himself open to checkmate. She had finally won. However, victory wasn't as satisfying as she had imagined it. The win only made her feel empty inside. When she returned to the lab the following Thursday, she discovered that Cedric was gone. She sat alone at the chess board, staring down at the clockwork fish, wishing the old man could defeat her just one more time.

***

In the morning Timbre awakens to something tickling her head. She sits up and sees Ohime holding one of the red tips of her tentacle between her fingers with a handful of shells in her palm. Timbre shakes her hair free from Ohime's grasp and glares at the girl who is smiling brightly back at her.

"So pretty," Ohime says.

Timbre's tentacles are covered in tiny cone-shaped seashells that Ohime had stuck to her while she slept.

"What the hell have you done to me?" Timbre bellows.

"Your tentacles are sticky," Ohime says, "You look like a warrior goddess."

Timbre groans, pulling the shells off of her. Ohime watches her and giggles.

"Get out of my sight before I throw a poison dart at you," says Timbre.

Ohime runs outside to explore more of the island. Timbre starts packing up supplies from the pantry. While she is putting cans of food into her fishnet bag she hears Ohime scream from outside. She sighs, thinking to herself *what is it now?* and regrets that she's taken the girl with her this far. Timbre runs out to Ohime to find her under a nori tree, staring down at a dead body.

The body has begun to rot, and has swollen to three times its normal size, like a blowfish. It is Cedric.

"Get away from him," Timbre commands Ohime.

The girl takes a few steps backward and almost loses her balance before running back inside the warehouse.

Timbre steps closer to Cedric's corpse. She wonders

what happened to him. Apart from being a rotting body he doesn't look harmed in any way. Perhaps his clockwork heart finally did give out on him. Timbre decides to dig a grave for him.

As she buries Cedric she remembers the times that she spent with him. She feels now that they were the happiest moments she had while working with Dr. Ichii. After he left the lab that day, she never saw him again. He had sent word to her that he was living in Ghoshi Territory and he said if she ever needed anything she could come to the island in the middle of the pink swamp. She's happy that she found him here, but she wishes that she would have come sooner.

CHAPTER SEVEN

Even though they had packed everything they could carry, half of their supplies were already depleted by lunch time.

"We're almost already out of food," Ohime says.

"Don't worry about it," Timbre says, "we will be to the bunker by nightfall. Then we won't have to worry about food or supplies ever again."

"We? You mean I'm allowed to stay?" Ohime asks through a big purple smile.

"I'll keep you around as long as you are useful. Do you have any skills?" Timbre asks.

The tips of Ohime's purple starfish point up quizzically.

"Are you good at *anything*?" Timbre asks again.

Ohime's eyes light up and she says, "Seashells."

Timbre shakes her head, "I mean something useful like cleaning or cooking. What did you used to do back where you came from?"

"I worked with seashells," says Ohime. "I was an apprentice seashell magician."

"What the hell are you talking about?" Timbre asks

"Seashell magic," Ohime says opening her crabshell purse. "Here let me show you." Ohime takes a handful of shells out of her purse and lays them down on a rock in front of her. She takes one of the shells and holds it out to Timbre. "Moon shells are for purification. Drop this in water or eat food out of it and you'll never get sick."

Timbre refuses to take it from her.

Ohime sets it down and takes another shell from her collection and holds it up. "Limpets are for courage, confidence and physical strength." She puts down the limpet and points at the shells next to it. "Lightning whelks promote dramatic positive changes and olive shells are for healing." Ohime smiles and points at the next shell, "Clams are for love, friendship and good relationships. Give half the shell to someone you love and they'll never leave you."

Timbre looks at her skeptically.

"The cone shells I stuck to your tentacles were for protection."

"That is just dumb," Timbre says. "Do you really believe in that stuff?"

"It is real," Ohime says, tucking the shells back into her purse. "It's not required that you believe in it."

***

Several hours later they arrive at a cluster of sand dunes. In the middle of one is a rusted door mostly covered in sand. "Our worries are over. This place will have everything we could possibly need." Timbre says, quickening her stride. Ohime follows close behind, clutching her crabshell purse close to her chest.

The door, as well as the walls, is constructed with reinforced steel. The once impenetrable shelter inside the dune is now abandoned and the door swings easily open with Timbre's kick. Inside is dark and hot like an oven. Ohime's pulse quickens with anticipation as Timbre's fingers fumble for the lights. A network of tubes lines the ceiling of the room similar to the ones in the Salty Hag, but the tiny blue fish that usually illuminate these tubes are all dead. In the dark, Timbre searches the room feeling along the shelves and tipping over barrels. After several minutes of awkward searching she determines there isn't a single thing on any of the shelves or inside any of the barrels. There's nothing here. The entire bunker is empty.

"I don't understand," Timbre says, "This place was supposed to be filled with food, weapons, and all kind of shit." She continues feeling around for a few minutes and then starts screaming. "What the fuck!" She stomps around on the ground. "All of this for nothing!"

Ohime comes up to Timbre and holds out a lightning whelk like a magic wand. Timbre swats it out of her hand and gives Ohime a violent stare.

Ohime picks the shell up off the ground and puts it back into her crabshell purse. As she does this, she takes out one of the sea sponges.

"What are you going to do with that?" Timbre asks her, her voice getting more suspicious and pissed off.

Ohime blushes and says quietly, "Um, I need to change mine."

Timbre pauses, giving the girl a scrutinizing look.

"Wait a minute," Timbre says, "you're on your period?" Ohime nods.

Timbre starts yelling at her, "Why the fuck didn't you

tell me this sooner? Don't you realize how many predators there are out there that can sense your blood?"

The points on Ohime's starfish turn back and point down. She looks at Timbre not knowing what to say.

Then Timbre's eyes widen as she comes to a realization. "Back at the Salty Hag . . . Dr. Ichii . . . the shark man was sniffing for *you*, wasn't he?"

"I don't know," Ohime says bowing, her head, "I think so . . . maybe."

"Goddamn it!" Timbre says. "I knew I shouldn't have bothered with you. *Fuck.* The last thing I need is to get mixed up with Dr. Ichii again. I need to get the fuck out of here." Timbre kicks over an empty barrel and it breaks across the concrete floor. She shoves Ohime out of her way and walks toward the exit.

"Where are you going?" Ohime asks her.

"As far away from *you* as I can get," Timbre says as she walks out the door.

***

Timbre had been loyal to Dr. Ichii for several years because he had supplied her with a means of survival. She had complete respect for him and never questioned what he was doing. Even when Cedric pointed out that the implants were being used for mind control she refused to believe him until she saw it firsthand.

She saw it happen to Freya, her roommate. Freya was like a younger sister to Timbre. They weren't exactly friends but Freya looked up to Timbre as an older sister. They both had a similar past and came to be employed by Dr. Ichii for the same reason. But like sisters they had a rivalry.

Freya was always trying her best to outshine Timbre but she wasn't as tall, as nimble, or as strong. She wanted to prove to Timbre and Dr. Ichii that she could be just as good a fighter as Timbre, if not better. In order to gain an advantage, she focused on getting upgrades to her implants. Timbre was already a good enough fighter, her implant was designed to give her added endurance and didn't require many augmentations. But Freya would get new augmentations on a weekly basis.

With each new upgrade, Timbre could see a change in Freya. She became more cold and calculating and her personality became more like a machine. Before the upgrades, Freya was as obstinate and careless as Timbre. She was spicy, she would tell jokes and get drunk and speak out of turn. She would get angry and aggressive toward people just for the fun of it. But after the upgrades nothing got a rise out of her. The implants had made her compliant and obedient. All she cared about was following Dr. Ichii's orders. That's when Timbre knew that Cedric had been right and that Dr. Ichii was trying to take control of people through the implants.

At first, getting upgrades was voluntary. But one day, Dr. Ichii started making them mandatory. That's when Timbre realized she had to get out of there as soon as possible.

When Timbre finally understood what Dr. Ichii was doing, she felt completely lost and betrayed. The whole time that she had been working for him she thought she was the one using him, she realized then that it was really her who had been used. She vowed that she would never let anyone use her again. Had Ohime known that she was leading them to her the whole time? Ohime was just using Timbre for protection and had made this whole pointless quest even more dangerous with her presence. It was enough that the bunker turned out to be a bust, but Ohime could have gotten her killed. Timbre is furious that she let herself make such a stupid mistake.

She feels something jab her hip in the pocket of her eel skin clothing. Timbre reaches into the pocket and pulls out the sharp thing. It's half a clam shell. She looks down at it. What did Ohime say about clam shells? *Give half the shell to someone you love and they'll never leave you.*

"That stupid kid," Timbre says. Ohime must have put the shell into her pocket when she wasn't paying attention. Timbre turns around and looks back toward the bunker.

"Such an idiotic, hopeless, girl." Timbre says to the shell.

***

Timbre can't believe that she is going back for the girl as she crosses the sand dunes toward the bunker. She knows that she's making a stupid mistake. But for some reason the idea of Ohime alone with Dr. Ichii's men hunting her down bothers her. She looks down at the clam shell again and rubs her red swirl finger inside its smooth purple scalloped curves.

"Maybe this stupid shell really does work." Timbre says as she puts it back into her pocket. She thinks that she'll at least get Ohime back to civilization and find her someplace to hide before leaving her. There's no chance she'll be able to fend for herself.

As Timbre climbs up the last big sand dune she can hear voices on the other side. She crouches down and peeks over the edge to see Dr. Ichii and his whole gang are already there. The muscular grey shark man is pulling Ohime, kicking and screaming, out of the bunker into the open. His circular saw fin is spinning wildly on his back.

"Oh shit, I'm too late," says Timbre.

***

Ohime is shoved to her knees in front of Dr. Ichii. She notices the fat legs of his pants are lumpy under his shiny silver suit. The smell of Ichii's cigar smoke mixed with his rancid fishy flesh odor makes Ohime sick and she pukes on the ground in front of her. The puke narrowly misses Ichii's shiny silver shoes but he doesn't move his feet a single inch. He looks down at her, his eyes extending from two long fleshy stalks with eyeballs inside the barnacle shells attached to the end of each one. The shells open and close when he blinks. His skin is entirely covered in parasitic barnacles, their hard calcium carbonate shells rough and crusty. Some of the barnacles ooze pussy goo that drip and harden on his face like stalactites.

"You took us all the way out to Ghoshi Territory looking for you," Dr. Ichii says to Ohime, "I might have to cut off your pretty little fingers for being such an inconvenience."

Ohime doesn't say anything. The shark man stands behind her, the whirring sound of his circular saw fin quickens.

"Where is it?" Dr. Ichii asks her.

Ohime bows her head to avoid looking at his diseased face.

"We know you have the coordinates and you're going to give them to us or you're going to die." Dr. Ichii says.

The shark man yanks on her pigtails and pulls her head back so Ohime is forced to look at Dr. Ichii.

Dr. Ichii bends down and exhales his cigar smoke in her eyes.

Ohime flinches and says, "I can't give you the coordinates. You're bad people. Only nice people are allowed to go."

Dr. Ichii laughs at her. "Hear that Vito? We're bad people."

The shark man snaps his jaws at Ohime.

"You're such a cute little starfish girl, aren't you?" says Dr. Ichii.

"Cute and tasty," says the shark man.

Dr. Ichii laughs with his henchman. "You should know that Vito here likes the taste of starfish. He's been smelling you for days and he is very hungry."

The shark man drools over her and unhinges his jaws so that his mouth is wide enough that he could swallow Ohime whole in one bite.

"If you don't tell me what I want to know I'm going to allow him to eat you," Ichii says. "One piece at a time."

Ohime shivers as she feels the shark man's hot breath against the side of her face.

"So what do you say?" Ichii asks. "Will you tell us?"

Ohime looks him in his gooey eyes, cowering under the breath of the shark man. All of her muscles cringe up as she gives her answer.

"I can't," she says. "You're not nice."

Ichii laughs at her.

"Very well," Ichii says. Then he turns to the shark man. "Vito, eat that stupid starfish off of her head."

When the shark man opens his jaws, Ohime yanks her hair free from the shark man's grasp and squirms out of

68

the way on all fours. But Vito lunges out and grabs her wrist, jerking her to a standing position. She flails wildly, kicking at him to get away. He laughs and holds her in place by one wrist. She tries to run, the broken heel of her shoe slips along the sand, and she runs in place with his strong grip holding her back. Vito watches her hungrily and seems even more excited by her struggle, his saw-fin whirring loudly and his mouth opening even wider.

She looks back at him and at his grey rubbery hand on her wrist. Her fingers start to feel numb from the pressure of his grip cutting off her circulation. She runs around behind the shark, twisting his arm backwards, and jumps onto his circular saw.

She doesn't make a sound as the saw tears through flesh and bone, slicing her arm off just below the purple ribbon on her puffy sleeved blouse. Blood sprays everywhere.

Vito, who is still holding her wrist, looks down at the severed arm in shock and surprise. Then he drops the arm, turns around and reaches out to grab her. She ducks, scurries under him and crawls between his legs. He bends down to catch her but she quickly grabs her severed arm and runs off before he can get hold.

Ohime's eyes are filled with fear and pain, but the adrenaline racing through her body gives her speed. She has to find a way out of here. She doesn't stop running and doesn't look back as she darts between two henchmen who are too busy laughing hysterically at what just happened to even try to grab her.

Dr Ichii screams, "Grab her!" His eye stalks protrude out in anger.

Vito starts to run after her, but then a red figure summersaults from the top of the dune and lands in front of him in a three-point stance. Everyone stops, surprised by Timbre's entrance. She stands up slowly and tosses her tentacles out of her eyes with a flick of her wrist.

"What's this?" Dr Ichii says, his cigar hanging from the corner of his mouth. "Timbre, what the hell are you doing here?"

At the sound of Timbre's name, Ohime stops running and ducks into the shadows lining the side of one of the dunes and crouches down, cradling her severed arm.

Timbre says, "I'm here to protect her."

Ichii's men laugh at her.

Ichii smiles wide. "My, my, aren't you something? I always admired your spirit, Timbre, but your reasoning has always been flawed. On your own, you've always made dumb decisions. You should never have left me. Without me, you are nothing. You are trash."

"I'd rather be trash than a brainwashed slave," Timbre says.

Ichii's eyes narrow.

"I've had enough talking," Ichii says and then turns to a puffer fish man standing behind him. "Kill her."

The man steps forward, puffing out his chest, and sharp metal spikes pop out, covering his entire body. Before he can take another step, Timbre cuts him in half with a toss of her tentacled head.

"Everyone," Ichii bellows, grinding his foot on the ground to extinguish the stub of his cigar, "kill her!"

Timbre grabs Ohime from the shadows and runs.

***

Timbre and Ohime run through the sand dunes as fast as they can, but Timbre's stilettos sink into the sand, slowing her down. Even at the slower pace, Ohime's short legs and the broken heel of her shoes make it hard for her to keep up. They run for several hundred yards, but Ohime keeps falling over and has trouble getting up with only one arm.

Timbre yanks Ohime up by her pigtails and throws her over her shoulder so she can continue running. Vito and Dr. Ichii's entire army are following close on their trail. On the other side of the dunes, they enter a coral reef.

The reef is a labyrinth. Its walls tower above them and it's difficult to know which direction won't lead to a dead end. Timbre darts between clusters of blue spiral wire coral as tall as buildings and giant pink brain coral. The twists and turns and tiny passageways are perfect for dodging their pursuers. Timbre glances over her shoulder and can tell that the henchmen are spreading out, attempting to cover the entire area. Despite Ohime's bulk and weight, Timbre continues carrying her with surprising agility. Ohime hugs tightly onto her back, still holding onto her severed arm.

As they round the next corner, they are stopped by one of the henchmen. He has a seahorse head, large muscular legs and a spiky metal seahorse tail implant.

The seahorse man raises his tail behind him like a scorpion and it shoots razor blades at their necks. Timbre dodges and the blades stick into the coral walls around them, breaking off bits of shells that rain down into Ohime's hair.

Timbre drops Ohime and spins around quickly, covering the seahorse man in poison darts. He falls to the ground paralyzed and Timbre picks Ohime back up and keeps running.

The next path she chooses is covered in seagrass hanging from the top of the coral walls like a curtain. She steps through the curtain and Ohime swings her severed arm back and forth like a machete to keep the grass from engulfing them completely. Once they are through the grass they reach a deep ravine with a river running through the bottom of it.

"Oh great," Timbre says as she skids to a stop at the edge of the ravine. "We can't go back. We're going to have to find a way over."

She scans the area for another way to escape. Suddenly, something metal spins through the grass and cuts off one of Timbre's tentacles. She screams and looks back. It's Vito.

He's released his saw-fin like a shuriken and another appears on his back in its place. Ohime hugs tighter to her back, withdraws an olive shell from her purse, and sticks it to Timbre's severed tentacle.

Vito makes his way over to them just as Timbre spots a land bridge a few yards to her left. She runs over to the bridge, the shark man still in pursuit throwing circular saws at her as fast as he can.

When she reaches the bridge, Vito catches up to her. She can smell Ichii's cigar smoke on his sickly grey skin. His muscles bulge out and he lunges at her, his mouth open wide.

"Vito," Timbre says, "come to your senses. He's controlling your mind."

Vito throws more saws at her and she dodges.

"Don't lecture me, you whore," Vito says. "What happened to your loyalty?"

Timbre releases her darts, but they miss.

Vito releases another saw-fin and as Timbre ducks, Ohime falls off of her back. Before Timbre can catch her, she goes over the edge of the bridge. Ohime screams as she falls and drops her severed arm, then reaches out with her remaining arm to grab a hold of the giant stalk of a sea flower protruding from the edge of the cliff. Her fingers slip, but she gets a grasp, dangling there precariously. At any moment, she feels that she could drop into the rapid waters below.

Timbre tries to reach for Ohime but the shark man rushes her and knocks her over. She leaps to her feet and jumps over him. Vito turns and snarls at her with all of his sets of teeth. Timbre lunges forward, whipping her tentacles around in a semi-circle, but Vito quickly jumps out of her range.

Timbre cartwheels through the air, lands on the other side of the bridge, and looks down at Ohime dangling from the flower. She reaches down and grabs the girl's arm but as she lifts it up she realizes it is the one not attached to Ohime's body. She looks confusedly at the dismembered limb for a moment, then drops it on the ground.

Before she can reach down again, Vito crosses over the bridge and jumps on top of her back. The two tumble across the ground, its rough coral surface causing tiny lacerations all over both of their bodies. Timbre jumps to her feet and the shark man reaches out for her leg, but Timbre sticks the spiked heel of her shoe through his eye. He screams and falls back. She turns her head like a windmill and her tentacles cut through his body, chopping him to grey chunky pieces.

Timbre steps through the chunks of Vito and grabs Ohime from the edge of the cliff, pulling her to the top. Ohime rubs dirt from her dress as she gets to her feet. Looking back at the land bridge, Timbre reaches down to retrieve the shark man's circular saw fin still whirring on the ground. The chunks of flesh vibrate in her hand as she holds the saw blade in front of her.

Ohime looks across to the other side of the bridge and can see Dr. Ichii and the rest of his men making their way through the seagrass curtain. Timbre takes the saw and cuts through the end of the land bridge, causing it to collapse. Like an earthquake, the sliding rocks thunder through the earth as the land bridge crumbles to pieces.

Dr. Ichii and his henchmen stand on the other side of the ravine watching the collapsing bridge. They look at her, unable to cross, their eyes filled with rage. Freya pulls out her bow and attempts to shoot arrows across the ravine at them, but the distance is too great. Timbre flips them off.

"There won't be another way across this ravine for miles," Timbre tells Ohime. "Plus, with Vito dead, they won't have as easy a time tracking us."

Ohime reaches down and retrieves her severed arm from the ground and cradles it like a baby. They walk off, leaving Dr. Ichii stranded across the divide.

CHAPTER EIGHT

Several hours after crossing the ravine Ohime and Timbre arrive at a small cave. They have to climb up the steep coral wall to get to it, but once inside and away from anything they finally feel safe.

Timbre gathers some bullwhip kelp and starts to prepare a salve for her wounds. Once she is done applying it to herself, she turns to Ohime. Timbre takes the severed arm from her and carefully inspects the stump at the end of her shoulder.

"I'm so sorry," Timbre says.

"It's nothing," says Ohime.

"What do you mean it's nothing? You lost your arm. There's nothing I can do to help you."

Ohime smiles, "It will grow back!"

"What are you talking about?"

"I'm a starfish girl," Ohime says. She takes some olive shells out of her purse and she rubs them on her shoulder. "I can use magic remember?"

Timbre inspects the girl's shoulder stump more closely

and sees the tiny bud of a new arm already re-growing.

"What?" Timbre says. "That's . . . interesting."

The baby toe-sized arm grows from her stump. Timbre is both shocked and amazed by the girl's regeneration ability.

"I'm glad you're okay," she says. "But now you are going to tell me why Dr. Ichii is after you."

Ohime's starfish turns a darker purple and she stares at the ground. "He's a bad person," she says.

"I know, I used to work for him."

Ohime looks up at her with lavender tears forming in her eyes. "I told you my parents are dead," she says. "They died in a fire."

"Who were your parents?"

"They were ecologists. They were trying to help people. Their research had shown that it is safe for people to live on the surface of the plant again. Their plan was that a team of scientists from Pod-9 would travel to the surface to investigate and if everything was fine they would establish a new colony and help get everyone out of the dome."

"Travel to the surface? What are you talking about? No one leaves the dome. How were they going to do that?"

"My parents have a ship. It belonged to my great-great-grandfather a long time ago. We were going to use the ship to get to the surface. That's why Dr. Ichii is after me. I am the only person who knows where it is."

"What happened to the team of scientists?"

The lavender tears slip out the corners of Ohime's eyes, "They all died. I am the only person who survived the fire." She takes her severed arm nestles it in her crabshell purse.

"So are you going to tell me where the ship is?"

"Ninkasi Territory."

Timbre raises her eyebrows. "That's the most dangerous territory in the dome. It was completely cut off after the volcano erupted years ago."

"Before my parents died, they told me to gather nice people and take them to the ship. They only want nice people living in the new colony. Not bad people like Dr. Ichii."

Ohime looks into Timbre's eyes for a few moments and says, "Nice people . . . like you."

"I'm not a nice person."

"Yes, you are."

Timbre changes the subject. "Even worse, in order to get there, you have to cross through Kujira Territory and Nanohana Territory. A trip to Ninkasi would be suicide."

"So you won't go?" asks Ohime

Timbre looks down at the girl, her blood splattered dress, her missing arm, her glossy eyes.

"I didn't say that," she says.

"So you'll go?"

"I didn't say that either," Timbre says.

Ohime lowers her eyes and the two sit in silence for what seems like hours.

Timbre is tired of this wild goose chase. She doesn't know whether to trust this girl. Ohime's parents might have told her some crazy stories and there's no way to know if any of this is really true. But she knows that the problem with the yellow algae is only getting worse. Without the implant upgrades she'll end up going crazy just like the rest of the mutants. And the option of becoming one of Dr. Ichii's puppets like Freya is out of the question. So, she decides that she will help Ohime, but she has to be cautious. With Ichii on their trail, the task isn't going to be easy.

"Get some sleep." says Timbre. "We have to get moving again in a few hours. It's safest to travel through Kujira at dawn."

"So you'll go with me?" Ohime says, the tips of her starfish pointing straight up.

"You better not be wrong about this."

CHAPTER NINE

Timbre has heard stories about Kujira Territory. Even before the collapse of their government, she had been warned against coming to this place. It has taken most of the day to get here, but Timbre and Ohime finally reach the edge of Kujira. There is no sign of Dr. Ichii and his men, but Timbre knows it won't be long before they catch up. Vito was Ichii's best tracker, but not the only one he employed. In attempt to throw them off their trail, she had Ohime throw her used tampon sponges in random directions along their way here. Hopefully that will keep Ichii guessing long enough for them to make it through Kujira, but first they have to make it past the entrance.

The entrance to Kujira is the mouth of a tunnel at the base of a steep mountain. When they arrive at the tunnel they discover it has been blocked off. Giant heaps of rusted metal welded together obstruct any further travel and the walls of the mountain are unscalable. Timbre inspects the hunks of rust attached to the entrance of the tunnel.

"We'll have to break through."

She starts tearing away salt-crusted shards of the heavy sheet metal.

"What's so dangerous about this place?" Ohime asks.

"Nobody knows," says Timbre. "Anybody who has gone into this territory has never come back. It's been closed off for years. When I was a kid, the guy that ran the corner store on my block was ex military. He told me a story about Kujira that I'll never forget. He said that a platoon had been deployed to secure the area and when they didn't report back after two hours, he was sent in to investigate. He made it halfway into the tunnel before he saw the piles of bones scattered on the ground at the other end. Human skeletons in the number of the platoon. The bones were completely white, not a single piece of flesh left on them nor a single drop of blood. It rattled his mind to think what could have happened. He didn't want to be a coward but he knew that he didn't stand a chance against whatever had annihilated the entire platoon. He ran all the way back to his camp and when he told the officials what he had seen the army barricaded the entrance. Since then, I haven't heard of another person setting foot in Kujira."

Timbre pries a giant piece of the rusted metal loose with her red-swirled fingers. It takes all her strength but she's able to crack open a section of the barricade wide enough for them to slip through.

"I guess we'll find out now," Timbre says.

Ohime clutches onto a cone shell with her small fist. She still carries her severed arm tucked into the side of her crabshell purse.

The tunnel is dark and smells like mixture of rust and rotten fish. Timbre walks confidently through the tunnel as if she can see in the dark and Ohime tries her best to keep up, stepping gingerly over bones and pieces of broken metal.

Once they are through the tunnel the landscape opens up into a vast wasteland of sand and bones. Giant whale skeletons litter the ground in every direction as far as they can see. At one time, this area was an integral part of the biodome ecosystem with a vast sea filled with whales. But the sea had dried up decades ago and now it is just a graveyard. The bones rise above them like buildings, white spirals, loose bones.

Ohime approaches one of the skeletons and touches her palm to the side of its smooth white surface. A tear rolls down her cheek.

"This is a sad place," says Ohime.

She looks around and notices the skeletons of other creatures, bright red crabshells, blue spiral turtle shells, and some bones that look human. She bends down and starts stacking bones and shells on the ground, arranging them into a circle.

"What are you doing?" Timbre asks.

"Their spirits are trapped here," says Ohime. "I have to help release them."

"We don't have time for that," Timbre says, motioning forward with her head.

Ohime follows her.

Timbre moves quickly but keeps looking over her shoulder to the left and the right.

"What's wrong?" asks Ohime.

"I feel like we're being watched," says Timbre. Out of the corner of her eye, she sees movement in the distance. Then she notices that Ohime has stopped again to erect another seashell monument.

"We have to keep moving," Timbre says, tugging on one of Ohime's pigtails.

***

Ohime and Timbre reach the whale refinery. This place is very old and crumbling at its foundation. Years ago whaling was a booming industry in the dome. This is where sperm whales had once been herded from the sea; holes were poked in their big heads to allow the liquid fat to drain out into barrels and used as fuel for lamps, lubricant, and heat. When the economy collapsed, this refinery had been abandoned and now only the whitened bones of the whales were left, creating a spooky labyrinth of giant skeletons. Among them roam coffin fish, walking along on their tiny legs between the dark shadows with glowing lures on their heads like lanterns.

The building is constructed out of bones. It towers above them like a morbid cathedral. At the very top of one of the spires they can see a cable extending out across what used to be a vast sea. This aerial tramway used to shuttle workers in from Nanohana by cable car, and Timbre thinks that if they can make their way up to it there might be a chance that they can get the car working which will take them all the way across the deserted sea.

Timbre hesitates when they get to the bottom of the structure.

"What's wrong?" asks Ohime.

"The only problem is that we have to go through the building to get to the tramway," says Timbre. "I'm not excited about going in there. There's no telling what we're going to run into. We'd better move quickly."

82

Once they enter the building, they find it's piled with more bones. The bones here are mostly human and not just scattered around haphazardly, but are stacked neatly in piles that look like little doll houses within the corridors.

"This is what I was afraid of," says Timbre. "Whatever creatures are out here are using this place as their shelter. We have to move quietly. Be really careful."

Timbre and Ohime creep through the corridors. Ohime tiptoes around the bones and tries her best to keep up with Timbre. They hear movement up ahead, so Timbre leads them down a different hallway. They come to a ladder leading up to the rafters.

"It will be best for us to climb up," Timbre whispers. "We have to make it to the zipline."

Ohime looks at the ladder and then down at her severed arm dangling out of her crabshell purse. Timbre realizes that Ohime is going to have some trouble climbing up with only one arm.

"Climb up on my back," Timbre tells her while bending down to let Ohime take hold. She notices that Ohime's new hand is already starting to form. At the end of the little bud of re-growth, there is a hand the size of a pinky with its little fist in a ball the size of a rosebud.

They scale the ladder and reach the narrow bone rafters. Timbre squats down again and says, "You'll have to walk on your own up here, it's too narrow for me to balance while carrying you."

Ohime carefully walks along the narrow bones following closely behind Timbre. They wind their way through the rafters for several minutes and then Ohime hears a noise below.

She looks down and sees two small figures darting

lightning-fast through the hallway below. They are badly mutated but she can tell they are only children. The creatures are chasing some kind of small animal that is scurrying to get away, their skittering feet echo in the hallways.

Timbre turns around and holds her index finger up to her mouth, motioning for Ohime to be quiet.

Ohime is too scared to move or even breathe. Frozen in place, she watches as the children catch the animal with their fish mouths, their razor sharp teeth tearing it apart quicker than she can blink. In seconds, the furry creature is reduced to a skeleton, its white bones sucked clean. Then the children continue on down the hallway and round another corner out of sight.

Ohime lets out her breath and feels grateful that the children didn't look up to the rafters. Timbre turns her head and notices that Ohime hasn't moved. She motions urgently for Ohime to follow. The longer they linger, the more likely they will be discovered.

Around the next corner Ohime looks down and sees a pile of snoring, sleeping bodies. They are mostly human but they have fish heads with giant eyes and bulging underbites that show off their razor sharp teeth.

"Piranhas," Timbre whispers. "Be careful not to wake them." Then she climbs to the next rafter.

Ohime reaches into her crabshell purse, pulls out a cone shell, and holds it out in front of her like a dagger.

Timbre gives her an evil look. She wishes that the girl would stop with the stupid shell shit. Frustrated, she reaches out to grab the shell out of Ohime's hand and accidentally knocks it out of her grip. It clatters on the ground. The sound awakens the piranha people. All at once, dozens of eyes point up at them. Threatening mouths gape wide with snarling teeth.

"Run!" Timbre yells.

The piranha people start shrieking. Some of them try to scale the walls but the bone is too smooth for them to climb. The two of them run across the bone rafters and see a doorway up ahead. They make it through the doorway and are able to lock it shut before any of the piranhas catch up to them.

They've made it to the aerial tram room.

***

Timbre fidgets with the motor of the tram for several minutes, but kicks the side of the car.

"Shit, it's completely broken."

Outside the door they can hear the shrieking of the piranhas. The sound is deafening. Scraping and scratching against the metal door.

"What's that?" Ohime asks, pointing at a heap of metal in the corner.

Timbre steps over to investigate and discovers that it is a two-seat, foot-pedaled cable bicycle.

"They must have used this thing for maintenance when the tram was down," says Timbre while investigating it. "It looks like we might be able to hook this thing up to the cable, but I can't guarantee it will hold."

This bike looks like a piece of junk. It's old and rusted and the gears hardly turn at all. Timbre works fast and Ohime covers her ears to try and block out the shrieking.

Just as they are able to get the bicycle connected, the door breaks down behind them. Ohime and Timbre jump on the bike and pedal out into the open.

***

High above the ground, Timbre and Ohime pedal their way across the zip line over the graveyard of bones.

"This thing feels like it's going to fall apart at any second," Ohime says, while clutching tightly to the handlebar with her good arm.

"Just keep pedaling," Timbre says.

Ohime looks down at the bones below. At first there is nothing, then she sees movement, then she can make out shapes of bodies. But they are not piranha people—they are Dr. Ichii and his henchmen.

"There they are!" Ohime hears the blue mohawk woman say.

"Shit!" says Timbre

Ohime starts pedaling faster, trying not to let the broken heel of her shoe slip off the pedal.

The blue woman starts shooting arrows up at them. The arrows are tipped with sharp piercing spiral shells that spin like drills. A couple of the spinning arrows whiz past Ohime. One of them snags the ribbon in her hair, tearing it away from her head.

"Faster!" screams Timbre.

Ohime is out of breath and struggling just to hold on. The bike creaks loudly and the chain clatters as if it's about to fall off. Timbre doesn't look down and keeps pedaling.

Suddenly the volley of arrows stops. Then they hear the shrieking. Ohime looks down and sees that the piranha people emptying out of the whale refinery, attacking Ichii and his men. Turning away from Timbre and Ohime, Dr. Ichii orders his men to take defensive positions. Freya shoots down two of the piranha men with her drill-like arrows, but the mutants are too fast for most of them. Ichii's men scream in fear as razor sharp teeth shred their flesh down to the bones.

Ohime keeps pedaling, the bike rattling violently across the cable. She looks back over her shoulder and realizes that the piranha people are crawling across the cable after them.

"They're on the wire!" Ohime says.

The piranha's mouths chomp-chomp at her as they scale the cable toward the bicycle, splattering bloody foam from their long razor teeth.

"Just ignore them and keep pedaling," Timbre says.

"They're too close," says Ohime. "They're going to catch us!"

Timbre looks back, tossing her hair over her shoulder with a twist of her neck, releasing poison darts into the piranhas on the wire. The piranha people fall to the ground, paralyzed.

Then Ohime's foot slips and one of her pedals comes loose and falls off, dropping to the ground below. The bike saddle under Timbre's butt breaks in half, the handles separate from the frame, and the chain makes a loud screechy sound.

"The bike's falling apart," Ohime yells.

Timbre pedals faster, ignoring the broken parts. "We're almost there."

Ohime looks down to see several skeletons lying across the sand, some of them still posed in mid-stride, their bones stripped clean of their flesh before they could even fall over.

Two-thirds of Ichii's army has already been killed by the creatures. The survivors fight on, back to back, but they are completely overwhelmed. A new soldier falls to the piranhas every few seconds.

"I don't think Ichii is going to make it out of there," says Ohime.

"Good riddance," says Timbre.

As they cross over the barricade into Nanohana Territory, the ground drops away. Ohime looks down past her rocking horse shoes at a canyon so deep that the ground cannot be seen, covered in a purple mist. The starfish girl's eyes light up at the colors of the valley below, forgetting the fact that their bicycle is still falling to pieces.

The back chain breaks from the zip line, and the back half of the bike falls back into a vertical position. Ohime drops from her seat and grabs hold of Timbre's tentacle hair, her feet dangling into space.

"Hold on!" Timbre says, as she pedals the bike from their vertical position.

With only the front wheel remaining attached to the zip line, they move much slower, only inches at a time. The bike continues to fall apart. Ohime looks down to see bits of metal and gears plummeting into the bottomless canyon below.

When they get close enough to the platform, Timbre tells Ohime to hold tight to her back as they jump across the divide. Just as they leap from the bike, the front wheel snaps from the zipline and the bicycle falls. They imagine themselves still on the bike as it disappears into the purple mist below.

At the other end of the platform, the cable continues across the canyon, but here it is covered in seaweed fashioned into a rope bridge.

CHAPTER TEN

Ohime and Timbre have been walking for hours on the seaweed rope bridge that stretches across the canyon, but they still can't see the other end of it. They have to step carefully with one foot in front of the other, balancing like tightrope walkers on the cable with the assistance of only shifty seaweed railings. The mountains forming the canyon have striations of deep reds and purples like muscle tissue. The canyon still seems bottomless and the muscle mountains stretch far out into the distance.

Ohime looks down and sees swirls of red and purple mist licking her toes. Her stomach has cramped up and she has a hard time breathing. She is worried that she will fall at any moment, but does her best to maintain balance with just one arm and a broken heel shoe. Ohime thinks that climbing across this bridge might be the scariest thing that she's ever had to do. Scarier than Dr. Ichii and the piranha people combined. But she must press on, they have to keep going.

"How much further does this bridge will go?" Ohime asks Timbre, who is walking catlike in front of her, completely relaxed as if walking along cables is a perfectly natural thing for her to do.

"This cable was once used for transporting people across the territory," Timbre says. "The aerial tram was the old form of public transportation. There must be a stop along the line eventually."

After a while further, the mist below them clears and stretched out below them at the bottom of the canyon is a sea of yellow.

"Good god, the yellow algae is thick here," says Timbre

"It looks like a golden ocean," says Ohime.

At last they come to the end of the bridge and have to climb down a rope ladder to get down to land.

"Be careful, the yellow algae is everywhere," Timbre says, as she looks down at the yellow covered ground below the bridge. But once she gets down she realizes that it is not yellow algae. It is a great field of harmless yellow flowers. In fact, better than harmless, they are rapeseed plants, delicious to eat.

"I found our dinner tonight," Timbre says.

"We're going to eat the yellow algae?" Ohime asks.

"No, I know why this place is called Nanohana, it's the name of this plant. Nanohana is rapeseed, tender bitter greens."

Ohime plops down into the soft flowers and stuffs a handful of the yellow buds in her mouth. "Mmmm, the flowers are peppery," she says.

They climb up the red hill in front of them and find an abandoned house. The house has been completely overtaken by the nanohana plant. Yellow flowers burst out of every inch of the house, making it look like a float in a parade.

"It's so pretty," says Ohime and runs inside the house. Every square inch of the inside of the house is covered in the flowers as well. Ohime plops down on a fluffy bed of yellow and rolls around comfortably.

"We can stay here for the night," says Timbre. "We don't know what lies ahead and it will be better to wait until daylight for exploring."

"What about the bad people?" asks Ohime.

"Dr. Ichii and his men are dead," says Timbre. "We don't have to worry about them anymore."

***

Feeling much more refreshed in the morning, the pair make their way across Nanohana. The yellow flowers give way to muddy ground. They see the tops of giant clam shells amidst the mud and it makes Ohime smile.

"The clamshells look like doorways," Ohime says. "I wonder what's inside?"

She grabs a hold of Timbre's hand and squeezes it affectionately.

Timbre yanks her hand away and then notices that Ohime took hold of her with the hand that should have been missing. Her budding new arm has grown to the size of a baby's arm.

"Shit, your arm is really growing back fast," says Timbre.

"My shell magic is strong."

Timbre notices Ohime is still toting along her severed arm hanging out of her crabshell purse, but it is now getting lumpy and the hand is curling into a ball.

"Are you going to continue carrying that around with you?" Timbre asks. "It looks like it's starting to rot."

Ohime ignores her and bends down to touch one of the giant oval clam shells. As she strokes it until the shell opens up. Ohime peeks inside and sees a purplish fleshy blob covered in iridescent blue spots. She reaches out with one finger and pokes the soft flesh. It shifts and turns, until Ohime sees a face looking back at her. The face blinks its glowing blue eyes at her and opens its toothless mushy mouth, making a loud sucking sound.

Ohime stumbles back, startled, and bumps into Timbre who glares down at the blobby clam creature. Suddenly all around them, hundreds of giant clam shells open up. Their lights blinking on in succession until the mud flat glows blue in every direction. The giant clams aren't real clams at all, but a colony of mutant clam people. They all open their mushy mouths, the sucking sound cacophonous and deafening.

"Oh shit," says Timbre, as she sees the crazed look in their eyes.

She whips her head and poison darts fly out, but before the darts reach the soft bodies of the clam people their shells snap shut, shielding them. At least it clears a path to the edge of a mountain. Timbre pushes Ohime in front of her toward the red rocky hill. When they get there, it is too steep to climb, so Timbre lifts the starfish girl onto her shoulders to boost her up. Ohime is able to pull herself up to a ledge with mostly the strength in her longer arm. But once she is up there, she can find no way to help Timbre climb.

"I can't get to you," Timbre calls up to Ohime. She points to her right. "Go that way and I'll try to find another way up."

Ohime makes her way across the ledge. She thinks that

it's a good thing she has decent balance, especially with her broken shoe. But her stomach knots up again with fear.

The clam people behind Timbre have all opened up their shells again and are sticking long blobby arms out of the mud and pulling themselves toward her along the ground. The sucking sound is threatening. *Ssshluuuuck, sshluuuuk, sssshluuuuck.* Timbre cringes as a wave of pain passes through her temples. She releases her darts at the clams again but this time they close and open their shells quickly, like snapping mouths avoiding the darts. The army of clam people creep closer.

Timbre leaps into the air and windmill kicks two of the clam shells and they domino back into several others behind them. She darts through the opening and is able to slice into the purple flesh of three more of them as she summersaults. Her tentacles slice their flesh, causing their blue lights to flicker and go out. Timbre continues fighting off clam people, leaving a silent dark trail of corpses and shells in the midst of the glowing blue sucking swarm.

Ohime finds a hiding spot at the other edge of the cliff above and watches as the dance of lights and gore on the red rocks below makes the valley turn purple. She strokes the side of her severed arm, and sticks shells to the fingers that are curling like snails.

Timbre makes her way across the mud to another mountain and is able to leap up and catch the edge of a ledge. Before she can pull herself up, one of the clam people sucks her foot into its mouth. She thrashes around trying to paralyze or maim it, but it snaps its shell shut on her leg like a fish trap. She cries out at the crushing pain as the clam tightens around her limb. She can't pull herself up but grips onto the ledge with all her strength to avoid being dragged down into the mud. She tries to lift her leg with the shell on it, but the giant thing is bigger than she is and much too heavy.

She waits for the clam to open and tries kicking it with her other boot, but it just sucks her leg in further and her fingers stretch more desperately to hold onto the ledge.

Then, from up above, she hears laughing. She looks up and sees Dr. Ichii. Next to him are his only surviving henchmen: Freya, Igo, a swordfish man and a halibut face giantess.

"You took the slow road," Igo chuckles at her.

"Where's the girl?" Ichii asks through a puff of smoke.

"What the fuck?" says Timbre.

"Tell me where she is and I'll help you out of your predicament." Ichii laughs at her. The barnacles on his face rattling and knocking loose stalactites of puss that land in Timbre's tentacles.

"Fuck you," Timbre says.

"Give us the girl or die, bitch," Ichii says.

"Go to hell," says Timbre.

The clam on Timbre's leg opens slightly and she is able to pull herself forward for a second but Ichii stomps on her red swirl fingers and she screams out in pain. He lifts up his foot and she struggles to regain her grip on the ledge with bloody fingers. The clam gets a hold of her other foot; it is now sucking both of them into its wet slippery gullet. She can feel its warm goo through her eel skin pants as it sucks. The pressure is starting to cut off the circulation in the lower half of her body.

"We're wasting time here," says Dr. Ichii, and he motions to his henchmen to head down the trail in the direction of Ohime.

"Igo, you stay here and make sure that thing finishes her off," Ichii says to the eel man.

"No problem boss," Igo says looking down at her hungrily.

Ichii follows his other three henchmen down the trail.

***

"Hey old partner," Igo yells down to Timbre who is hanging from the cliff. "I've got no ill will toward you, so I was thinking, how about you and me make a deal?"

"I'm not your partner anymore."

"Ya, well let's say for old time's sake, you let me fuck you and I help you out of your little, um, jam."

Timbre shakes her head forward and releases poison darts at him. Igo dodges the darts, his sinewy red spotted body bending and twisting as an eel's.

"Whoa, loosen up," he says. "Your only problem is you were always so high strung."

Timbre knows she isn't going to last much longer. The clam is tightening around her legs and it has sucked its way above her knees now.

Igo squats down at the edge of the rock and flicks his tongue out at her. "Come on, my urchin," he says. "Wouldn't you rather have me sucking you than that thing?"

Timbre's lower half has become completely numb and she winces as the clam creature sucks its way up her thighs. "Okay," she says. "Okay, just help me, okay."

Igo leaps down on top of the clam shell and stabs his arm straight through the shell, smashing all the way through until Timbre can feel his hand against her ankle.

The clam shell opens and Timbre sees the gooey purple face of the creature scream out in pain. She slowly pulls her legs free. Pins and needles shoot through her lower body in a tingly sensation as her circulation is restored to her limbs.

Igo pounds the clam shell into the mud with his feet, making sure it's dead. The surrounding clam people sense him as a threat and their blue lights blink more rapidly until all of them close their shells and silently submerge themselves into the mud. He leaps back up to the top of the ledge as Timbre pulls herself up.

Timbre looks at Igo and then starts to throw her head to release more darts and cut him with her tentacle whips, but he thrusts his hand against her neck and pins her against the ground so she can't move her head. Timbre struggles to breathe and gasps for air, flailing her arms out to each side.

Igo grins at her. "You were always so hot when you were violent," he says.

Timbre scratches at him and tries to kick him off, but he's too strong for her. Her legs feel like jell-o and she can barely move them.

Igo continues holding her down and grinds his pelvis against hers through their clothes. The clam goo still covers her legs, making her slippery. He smiles, his undulating eel body sliding easily around on top of her.

He attempts to kiss her but she spits into his eye and clamps her lips shut. He gets mad and rips her pants off with his free hand, exposing her red swirl belly and tentacled crotch. Then he unzips the front of his pants to release his engorged penis. He violently thrusts his cock into her, ripping open her dry vaginal lips through her anemone pubic hair.

He presses his hand down tighter against her neck, choking her, and arches his back as he thrusts deeper inside of her, his penis hitting her cervix. She bucks against him, but his weight is too much for her to throw. He starts swirling his dick around inside her, the same direction as the swirl on her belly. Then he freezes. Waves of paralyzing pain shoot through his dick up to his brain. His eyes open wide. His dick goes limp. Timbre pushes his paralyzed body off of her and he lands on the ground with a dull thud. She stands above him looking down, a grin on her face. She slowly grinds the heel of her stiletto into his soft cock, crushing it beneath her shoe. It pops like a ripe seaweed pod.

"Stupid Igo." She laughs at him. "I told you the day you fuck me is the day you will die."

He lays there motionless, unable to even blink his eyes. Pain races through every nerve. She steps over his body and squats above his head.

"Do you like this flower?" she asks, hovering her anemone vagina above his face. "Because it is as deadly as it is beautiful."

She slowly lowers herself toward him.

"Do you know how anemones eat?" Timbre says, squatting down further until her crotch is right above his nose. "First, they sting their prey with their tentacles, paralyzing it."

The anemone tentacles between Timbre's legs spread out exposing the opening of her vaginal mouth.

"Then they pull their prey inside of them," she continues.

Igo's unblinking red eel eyes bulge out of his head as

Timbre sits on top of his face. He can't even scream as his thick gummy lips are torn from his face and pulled into Timbre's vagina. He tries to scream but only a gurgle escapes his throat.

"Ever since the yellow algae changed me into part sea anemone," she says, "I've been able to feed on men this way."

She puts her hand behind his head and shoves it deep between her thighs. His muscles twitch beneath her. When she pulls his face away, his nose and the flesh of his cheeks are no longer there, exposing bloody facial tissue.

"It's my secret weapon," she tells him, rubbing a finger down his bloody lipless mouth.

His face twitches, as if he is trying to pull away from her finger. Her pubic tentacles curl against his chin as she leans in closer.

"You know, I can eat an entire man with my vagina. One piece at a time." The tentacles lick the blood from his chin. "But I don't have time for that. Ohime needs me."

She withdraws to a standing position, but then notices a look of relief cross the eel man's face.

"Of course . . ." she says, staring down on him, "I haven't eaten all day. Perhaps I'll have a little more."

She sits down on his face.

"The rest of your head should be enough."

The eel man gurgles in pain beneath her as Timbre's sea anemone vagina devours him one layer of flesh at a time.

***

Ohime stays hidden, waiting for Timbre, not knowing

what else to do. It starts to get dark. Ichii's men have made it over to the mountain where she is hiding and Ohime is paralyzed with fear when she hears their voices on the other side of the trail.

"She has to be close by," says the swordfish man, his teeth chattering in anticipation.

Ohime shifts further into the shadows.

Dr. Ichii is so close now that Ohime can smell his cigar smoke. It tickles the back of her throat and she almost starts to gag when she feels a hand clasp over her mouth from behind.

***

Timbre climbs up the red muscle mountains in the direction of Ohime. She hears voices up above her and looks up to see someone's legs dangling over the ledge. Timbre leaps up and grabs the ankles of the person and heaves herself up. She flips over and squats on top of the unfamiliar person, then hears Ohime's voice.

"Stop!" Ohime screams. "Don't hurt him."

Timbre looks at Ohime and down at the person lying beneath her. It's a man. His orange face curls into a smile, his bright black eyes crinkling in the corners.

"Hi," he says.

"Who are you?" Timbre asks.

"He's a nice person!" Ohime says.

"Name's Jaffa," he says. "You must be Timbre. 'Hime's been telling me all about you."

Timbre lifts herself off of him. He sits up and brushes the red rock dust off his white and black striped suit, then walks over to Ohime.

"Step away from the girl or I'll paralyze you," Timbre says.

Jaffa holds his hands out, palms open and says, "Whoa, I come in peace. I'm only trying to help."

"He saved me from getting captured by Dr. Ichii," says Ohime, reaching out and grabbing onto his hand with her baby arm.

"Plus, I'm a clownfish," Jaffa says. "I'm immune to sea anemone poison."

"That might be true," says Timbre, narrowing her eyes, "but poison isn't the only way I can hurt you."

"I promise," Jaffa says, "I am only trying to help. My people have a settlement near here, I can take you back. We have food and shelter."

Timbre eyes him suspiciously but Ohime reaches out with her other hand and takes a hold of Timbre's red swirl fingers. The three of them walk down the path together, Ohime in the middle swinging their arms.

CHAPTER ELEVEN

Ohime, Timbre and Jaffa reach the settlement. It is lit up with seaweed strings of colored lights hanging between white bubble shaped buildings. The colors bounce off the clean white buildings in kaleidoscopic patterns as the trio wind their way through the streets. Nothing here is crumbling, everything seems well maintained and organized, unlike every other area Ohime and Timbre have seen in the dome.

"What is this place?" Ohime asks.

"Ataru, the makeshift capital of Nanohana," Jaffa says. "Back before the collapse, Nanohana was the agricultural center of the dome. We're farmers, peaceful folk."

He walks them through a twilight garden describing the plants to Ohime.

"This garden is special," Jaffa says. "These plants all glow in the twilight. I like to come here to imagine things."

"What kind of things?" asks Ohime, reaching out and running her fingers along the moon plants and the soft silver rabbit's ears.

"Like talking plants," he tells her. "I talk to these plants every day. Sometimes, I imagine I hear them talking back to me."

Ohime walks through an arbor covered in glistening

silver web of vines.

"What do they say?" she asks.

"They tell me to love more," he says. He smiles so brightly that Ohime thinks that his smile is what makes the plants glow and not the moonlight.

Jaffa knows everyone and everything about Ataru. He is excited to show them around because he tells them that they never get any visitors and it's been decades since anyone has seen anyone other than their own kind.

He leads them to the large bubble-shaped building in the center of town. It is made of wood and covered in ornate carvings and decorated with colorful stained glass. Inside, dozens of clownfish people are laughing, talking and dancing. On a small circular stage in the center of the room a petite orange-and-white-striped girl lies on her stomach playing a toy piano. She wears a tulle skirt and kicks her striped-stocking feet above her head. Behind her a zebra-striped man wearing a red zoot suit smacks two sets of large white bones between his fingers in each hand as a percussion accompaniment. The man in the suit nods to Ohime and spreads a big black-lipped smile across his teeth. He dances quick steps. Loose and jangly. The snaps and clicks of the bones roll and rumble inside of Ohime and she feels herself loosen and relax.

The piano girl starts to sing, her voice fierce and piercing. The song is joyful and painful all at once. It makes Ohime's heart ache with longing for her home, her family and her friends.

"This is the central meeting place," Jaffa tells them. We come here to party together and discuss things. We also eat our meals together in the adjoining bubble. He describes all of the people as he points them out one at a time.

"There's Cassandra, the healer," he says pointing at an orange-skinned woman wearing clothing made out of all different sorts of seashells. There are even shells woven into her dreadlocked hair, reminding Timbre of Ohime's seashell magic. Jaffa points out the artist, the tarot card reader, the poet, the massage therapist, the librarian, the apothecary, the teacher, and the mechanic.

"These are such nice people," Ohime says, squeezing Jaffa's hand with her baby arm.

"How many people live here?" Timbre asks.

"Sixty-seven."

"Are you all clowns?" Timbre scrunches her eyebrows at Jaffa.

Jaffa laughs. "Yes, I guess you could say that. But deep down, who isn't a clown?"

Ohime giggles.

"I noticed that it looks like no one has any implants," Timbre says.

"That's true," Jaffa says.

"How is that possible?" Timbre asks. "Why haven't you all succumbed to the madness?"

"Beats me," says Jaffa. "We just enjoy life while we can."

After dinner he takes them to a room where they can settle in for the night. As they walk, they see a tall woman walking very fast in their direction.

"This is Eugenia, our leader," Jaffa says as he introduces them.

Ohime waves her little arm at Eugenia who ignores her and says to Jaffa, "I don't have time for these people. I have emergencies to attend to."

She hurries on past them without any further acknowledgement.

"She's always like that," Jaffa says. "Don't mind her."

He holds something out to Ohime that looks to her like a cross between a shotgun shell and one of Dr. Ichii's cigars.

"Breathable chocolate," he tells her. "Try it."

Ohime takes it from him. "What do I do with it?"

"You put it to your mouth and inhale it," Jaffa says.

Ohime puts the thing to her lips and sucks a sharp breath of air inward. Her tongue becomes coated in the warm rich velvety flavor, slightly bittersweet. It's like breathing in a chocolate factory.

"Delicious," Ohime says.

***

The room they are given is inside of another bubble-shaped structure with layers of richly colored silk fabrics in reds and golds draped from the ceiling. The amber light and musk scented air is warm and inviting. There are lots of large plush pillows scattered on the floor. Lining the walls are candles, small bowls of water with flowers floating in them and figurines of goddesses. Ohime drops down on one of the cushions and stretches out. She takes her deformed severed arm out of her crabshell purse and lays it carefully in the center of its own pillow. Then she covers it in seashells.

Timbre sits cross-legged on the hard ground with her knees crossed and her back straight. She faces the entrance to the bubble with her back against the wall.

"Do you ever wonder what's up there?" Ohime asks. "Outside the dome on the surface, I mean?" She stretches out her arms and legs and lays flat on her back on top of the giant pillow to gaze up at the silk fabric draped across the ceiling like wings.

"Can't say I have," says Timbre.

Ohime rolls her ankles and wrists in circles. "My parents told me that the ship is programmed with the coordinates to take us to an island where we can start a new life."

"That's a nice fairy tale," Timbre says. "At first, when I agreed to help you I was just hoping there would be enough valuable parts I could salvage from that ship to cash in on. After the disappointment of that bunker, I've got nothing left to go on. But since Ichii's been so keen on capturing you, I'm starting to believe there might be some truth to your story."

Timbre hears voices outside their room and stops talking.

"I'm at my wit's end," says the voice.

"Eugenia, we need to stay calm about this," says a voice that sounds like Jaffa's.

"But without the barrier we are doomed," Eugenia says. "We will succumb to the yellow algae just like the rest of the dome."

"There are implants," says Jaffa.

"It is unacceptable for our people to pollute their bodies with technology. I will die before I see an Ataruan become a cyborg."

"But what other option do we have?" says the voice.

"We must find another sanctuary."

***

"Citizens," Eugenia says to the crowd of clownfish people gathered in the central bubble, "I want to start out by telling you there is no need to panic."

Voices are whispering to each other in fear and anxiety throughout the room.

"I have called us all together because we must discuss the future of Ataru," Eugenia continues. "Some of you may not be aware that the reason we have been able to contain the yellow algae for so long has had to do with the high nitrogen content in the soil of Nanohana." Timbre and Ohime stand near the back of the room and watch as people in the crowd hold each other. Some of them are crying. Jaffa and Eugenia are on the stage facing the crowd.

"I have recently learned that the nitrogen has been depleted to such a level that our land is no longer impervious to the spread of the algae. We need to explore alternatives before we lose the capacity to protect ourselves. I am committed to protecting our civilization, but I need everyone's cooperation."

"But the nanohana plant itself is what contributes nitrogen to our soil," says one of the citizens. "We should be able to just plant more."

"The bacteria that has been infecting our nanohana has gotten worse," says Eugenia. "At first it just caused the plants to wither, but now the plants are dying. The bacteria also kills new plants before they get a chance to blossom. We have no choice but to move our settlement into the canyon where the nanohana grows wild."

"We can't move to the canyon," someone says. "We would be defenseless there. We should move to a safer territory."

Another clownfish man says, "There is no place safer than here. I have traveled and seen the rest of the dome, and every other place is already overrun with the algae."

"We have no alternative," Eugenia says.

Then Ohime stands up and raises her hand. Eugenia ignores the child, but Jaffa tells her to speak.

"I know a way out of the dome," she says.

The room goes silent, everyone turns to look at her.

"My parents built a ship," she continues. "You are all welcome to come with me to the surface."

Most of the clownfish people have no idea what to make of the girl. A few of them become angry, as if the girl is lying and making a joke of their dire situation.

"Explain yourself girl," Eugenia says.

Ohime explains the situation to them, and after hearing her story they are still unconvinced.

"Why should we trust you?" Eugenia asks the starfish girl.

"Because I don't lie," Ohime says.

The crowd bursts into shouts and taunts, chastising the girl for her preposterous claims. Ohime tries to speak up for herself, but the mob drowns out her voice. They don't quiet down until Timbre stands and snaps her tentacles in the air, creating a loud sound like the crack of a whip. The clownfish people become silent, gawking at the tall sea anemone woman as she steps forward.

"I don't trust her either," Timbre says to the crowd. "I don't trust anyone. But she is our best hope for survival and I am willing to take the chance and find a way to survive than give up and succumb to the insanity. That is why I am putting my faith in her."

The crowd starts murmuring amongst themselves.

"Silence," says Eugenia, holding her hands up in the air to regain control of the crowd. "We shall discuss this amongst ourselves, as citizens of Ataru." She points at the strangers and then waves them toward the exit. "Wait outside until we have made a decision."

Timbre turns to leave. Ohime bows her head to Eugenia

and then follows Timbre outside.

***

A while later, Jaffa comes outside to talk to them.

"We have come to a consensus. We agree that the citizens of Ataru will follow you to the ship, Ohime."

Ohime radiates a big purple smile at him.

"The only problem is that the passage to Ninkasi Territory was blocked off years ago," Jaffa says. "In order to get there we are going to have to blast a hole through the mountain."

Jaffa looks at Timbre and smiles. "But, we've already assembled the team of people to do the work and it will take just a week to blast through."

"Well, you better get started," says Timbre.

He nods his head and walks away, joining a small crowd of people who have gathered in the hallway to discuss plans for the demolition.

"I don't like the idea of this blasting," Timbre says to Ohime. "It might attract the attention of Dr. Ichii if it goes on too long."

***

Ohime stretches out on one of the giant pillows in their room, dreaming about all the nice people she will be able to bring with her to the new world.

Timbre stares down at her with a concerned look. "You know there is only room for twenty people on the ship, right?" Ohime pauses and looks at her quizzically, the tips of her purple starfish turning out to the sides of her head.

Timbre says, "You told me that it was designed to take a team of twenty scientists to the surface for research."

"Ya, so?"

"That's twenty seats, we can't fit all sixty-seven of these people."

"We can try to fit everyone or we can take multiple trips."

"We have no way of knowing if we'll even be able to drive the ship let alone take multiple trips."

"We have to try. I know for certain that these are the nice people my parents told me to find. It is my duty to take them with me."

"You are going to have to leave most of them behind."

"No. We can take them all. There's got to be a way."

"Whatever you say," Timbre says. She's not too concerned at the moment. If the Ninkasi territory is as dangerous as she has heard that it is, there's no way that everyone is going to survive the trip anyway. They might be lucky if even a third of them survive.

***

A week passes and Ohime's arm has completely grown back to its normal size. It is like her arm was never missing. She sits on a giant lily-orange pillow in her room, sewing some little babydoll clothes. On the pillow next to her, where a week ago she placed her severed arm, is a dolly-sized version of herself. She coos to it in a soft voice.

"What happened to your arm?" Timbre asks, pointing at the baby doll. The thing wiggles and dances around naked on top of the pillow. It is a perfect miniature version of Ohime.

"It's my baby," Ohime says.

"How did your arm turn into a baby?"

"I'm like a starfish, remember?" Ohime says. "When a starfish loses a limb then that limb will grow into another starfish. That's what happened to her." She points at her miniature clone. "My severed arm has become another version of me."

"So that thing is going to grow into another Ohime?"

"Yeah."

"So I'm going to have to deal with two of you now?"

"We'll be like twins."

Timbre smacks her hand to her face. It was bad enough having to deal with one Ohime. This is ridiculous.

Ohime holds up the doll-sized outfit. It has purple bows and puffy sleeves just like her own clothes. "I am making it a dress for the party tonight."

"What party?" Timbre asks.

"We are all leaving tomorrow, so Jaffa is throwing a big going away party tonight and everyone is invited."

***

All afternoon people have been piling their belongings onto the circular stage in the center building. The objects are tied together in bundles with ribbons. The stage is crowded with clothing, trinkets, cushions, a stack of old photographs, the toy piano, a hydro-bike, seashells, a chest of intricately carved wooden drawers.

"What's going on?" Ohime asks Jaffa.

"This is the pyre for the ceremony. We cannot take our belongings with us so we are going to burn them."

A procession of people on jumping stilts wearing white

skin-tight costumes enters the building and dances around with white candles. Their faces are painted as skeletons and they move like puppets on strings, twisting and turning on their tall legs. One of them extends a hand down to Ohime and gives her a purple flower shaped like a star and then keeps dancing.

Ohime smiles and clutches the flower to her chest.

The women wear crowns of same purple sea flowers in their hair and the men have long spiky shells adorning their heads like horns.

A feast is spread out in the dining area and Ohime and Timbre gorge themselves on buttery lobster curry, jasmine rice, naan, fresh fruits, mint chutney, pickled sea cucumbers and spiced baby crabs.

After the meal, everyone starts to gather around the stage for the ceremony.

Euegnia stands in front of the group. "Citizens of Ataru, it is time for us to say goodbye to our home. We honor the past and are grateful for all of the blessings that this land has bestowed upon us. We destroy the old to make way for the new. By burning our possessions, we leave behind all of our regrets and fears. We welcome into our souls the hope and renewal that this journey brings. We cannot take our belongings with us, but the memories we treasure shall forever remain in our hearts."

She lights the base of the pyre. The flame spreads from the bottom of the pile, slowly at first and then suddenly the entire stage is engulfed in flames. The clownfish people dance barefoot around the fire. Some of them wear bells on their ankles that jingle as sparks fly out from the stage. Others play drums and bones.

Timbre hangs back against the side of the building

with her arms crossed under her breasts and watches people dancing. Their orange skin glows in the firelight. They dance fast and hard, banging their feet against the ground and waving their hands in the air. Their bodies swing like loose ribbons. Ohime and Jaffa emerge from the crowd dripping with sweat and holding hands. They walk to a bar near the entrance to the dining bubble.

"Try the Kelpie Ale," Jaffa tells Ohime.

"I've never drank any alcohol," Ohime says.

"No time like the present," Jaffa tells her with a wink. He pours her a glass of the foamy green liquid. Ohime brings it to her lips and wrinkles her nose at the smell.

"Go on, down the hatch," Jaffa says.

Ohime takes a sip of the drink and coughs after swallowing it. Her head feels a little dizzy and her vision spins the colored lights into star-shaped patterns. She stretches out her arms to her sides and twirls around in circles to the music. The doll-sized version of Ohime spins in circles next to her.

The two Ohimes wander around through the crowd. Everyone is moving. The music gets louder. A clownfish man with a large round belly dances with sidesteps holding his hands out to his sides and moving his neck in circles. His belly jiggles like a jellyfish. He almost steps on mini-Ohime, but the little starfish girl jumps up out of the way and Ohime catches her in her arms. Ohime strokes the top of the little girl's starfish with one finger and mini-Ohime beams a pearly purple smile at her.

"I am so happy we found these nice people," Ohime says to her baby. "When we get to the island we will start a new life. I will teach you about seashell magic and bog turtles and sewing and we will live in a house together. We can dance together every day and maybe someday we'll find cute guys to marry us and we'll live happily ever after."

Mini-Ohime wiggles around in Ohime's arms and crawls up to her shoulder.

"We'll grow to be little old ladies together and can have lots of starfish babies. We can open a shop and make the prettiest clothes anyone has ever seen."

An orange-skinned woman with glowing white eyes sits by the fire and motions with her index finger for Ohime to come over to her. The starfish girl steps closer to the woman and notices that her eyes are closed. The white eyes are painted on the closed lids. The woman is old and her flesh is wrinkled and sagging. She wears a garment made from plants that seem to still be alive. The plant clothing clings to her body, growing around it and from it.

"Give me your palm," the woman says. The white painted on eyes glow at Ohime.

Ohime extends her newer hand to her.

The woman grasps Ohime's palm and smoothes her wrinkled fingers over the tiny suction cups that coat the inside of Ohime's arm. Then she traces the lines in Ohime's palm with one fingernail. The sensation of the old woman's touch makes Ohime shiver.

"You have a strong hold on others," says the woman. "You will live a long life and love a great many people."

Ohime smiles at her and bows her head. She doesn't know if the woman sees her do this because she still has her eyes closed but for some reason Ohime thinks that she does. Mini-Ohime sits on Ohime's shoulder and traces the lines in her own palm with her tiny fingers.

***

Timbre likes the feeling of the wall massaging her back. She rubs against the sharp corner of a pillar to scratch between her shoulder blades.

Jaffa walks up to her, "Care to dance?"

"No."

Timbre stops rubbing against the wall, realizing it made her look like she was swaying to the music.

"Come on. It's time you had some fun," says Jaffa.

Timbre eyes him suspiciously.

Jaffa thrusts his glass of Kelpie Ale in her face and smiles his big black-lipped grin. Timbre takes the glass from him and takes a sip.

"You look like you could use some fresh air. Let's go outside," says Jaffa.

Timbre follows him onto the second story balcony. She drinks the rest of the Kelpie Ale in one sip before handing the empty glass back to him.

"I can't wait to see what the ship is going to be like," says Jaffa. "I've never even dreamed of going to the surface."

"I never dreamed there'd be anywhere free of the yellow algae," says Timbre, looking out at the tops of the glowing bubble architecture.

Jaffa puts the empty beer glass on the ground and does a little jig around it. Then he bows to Timbre and makes an exaggerated gesture with his arm in the air and holds out his orange hand to her, inviting her to dance.

Timbre takes his hand and he pulls her toward him then spins her around like a waltzing ballerina. Timbre's chili-pepper hair twirls around him without harming him.

***

A loud crash sounds outside the building. The music is replaced with the sound of screaming. Ohime looks around and Jaffa is nowhere in sight, and she doesn't know where Timbre is either. She starts walking toward to doorway to see what is going on, but she's stopped by a crowd of people running in the opposite direction.

Across the room, Ohime sees Jaffa and runs toward him.

"What's going on?" Ohime asks.

"We're being attacked," Jaffa says.

Timbre appears next to Ohime. "Quickly, follow me," she tells them and then ducks to the side of the room. Ohime's head still feels dizzy as she watches Timbre slash through the wall with her tentacles and step out into an alleyway behind.

"This way," Timbre whispers to Jaffa and Ohime, motioning for them to follow.

"Where are we going?" Ohime asks.

"To the tunnel," Timbre says. "Dr. Ichii and his men have caught up to us. It's time to leave, now."

"We need to warn everyone," says Ohime.

"There's no time for that," says Timbre. "We need to save ourselves." Timbre grabs Ohime's arm and drags her through the alleyway, sneaking behind the buildings.

All around them dozens of clownfish people are getting killed by Dr. Ichii's men. Ohime sees a swordfish man slashing clownfish people into halves as they flee.

Blood-covered people run in all directions. None of them have any weapons. Some grab pitchforks and try to fight back, but they are just target practice to Freya and her drilling arrows.

Dr. Ichii lights a new seaweed wrapped cigar in the

115

bonfire and stands in the center of the building, laughing as he watches his henchmen go fishing.

***

Inside the tunnel, less than three dozen clownfish people are regrouping. The rest of the citizens are either dead or still in the village, fighting off Ichii's men. When they get to the other side, into Ninkasi Territory, they use the last of their dynamite to blast the tunnel closed, leaving many of their friends and family members behind.

"That should hold them," Jaffa says after the tunnel collapses.

"Not for long," says Timbre. "These guys have been trailing us for a while and I know how resilient they are."

"You are the reason my people are dead!" Eugenia screams at Ohime.

"You need to calm down, lady," Timbre gives Eugenia a stern look.

"I never should have listened to you," Eugenia says. "There is no reason why those people should have died."

Ohime's heart feels like it's going to explode inside her chest. *Eugenia is right* she thinks to herself. *It is all my fault that those people died.* Ohime cradles her doll-sized version of herself tightly to her chest. Her head is spinning and she feels like she is going to be sick. Ohime runs away from the crowd and down a path.

She slips on a patch of orange oily grease and falls backward, landing hard on her tailbone. Then she starts crying like she's never cried before, crying for her family, for the scientists, for all the people who have gone crazy, all the people who have died. She feels like she's never going to stop crying.

"Cut it out," Timbre's voice says from behind her. The sea anemone woman comes over to Ohime. "It's not your fault those people died."

Ohime's starfish is the deepest color purple Timbre has ever seen it turn.

"And besides, we can only take twenty people with us to the surface so those people were dead anyway," Timbre says.

Ohime cries even louder.

"What I meant to say was, um . . ." Timbre pauses for a moment, looking into Ohime's tear-filled violet eyes. "Look, let's be honest here. The fact is, everyone is going to die. This whole goddamned place is doomed. The yellow algae will wipe us out in a matter of a few months and our savior, Dr. Ichii, is nothing but a madman. All of us, every single one of us, will die eventually if we stay here. But you are offering us hope. The ship, it can be our salvation. Because of you, we have the chance to live. But we can't do this without you. We need you to show us the way."

Ohime says, "But, Eugenia . . . the nice people . . . they all hate me now."

"Just ignore that. They will feel differently once we get to the ship and you have a chance to save them."

Ohime rubs the tears out of her eyes.

"So, come on. Are you good to go?" Timbre stands up and offers her hand out to Ohime to help her stand up. Ohime looks up and Timbre smiles down at her.

Ohime's face brightens. "Wow, you've never smiled before," she says.

Timbre quickly erases her smile.

"You're pretty when you smile," says Ohime, taking a hold of Timbre's hands.

CHAPTER TWELVE

Ninkasi Territory is different than Timbre had imagined it. She's been to pretty much everywhere in the dome during her time working for Dr. Ichii but no business was ever done in Ninkasi because of the lava fields. At the time the dome was built, the underwater volcano was dormant and no one knew about it. But back before anyone had ever even heard of the yellow algae there was the eruption of the Ninkasi volcano. It changed the underwater landscape forever. Some people believe that the volcanic eruption is what caused the mutation of the algae into the toxic plague that covered the land. Some believe that the yellow algae originated from Ninkasi.

The soft lava still moves and shifts, making this landscape unpredictable, uninhabitable. Why anyone would choose to construct a research vessel way out here seems unreasonable to Timbre.

Ohime carefully steps along one of the land bridges formed by the lava. The heat from the cracked earth makes this whole area misty and humid. The hair at the ends of her pigtails is starting to curl.

After several kilometers they come to the edge of the

dome where the glass meets the ground. Giant golden snail shells as big as skyscrapers cling to the inside of the glass, some of them move very slowly, almost imperceptibly sliding across the surface.

On the other side of the glass is the open ocean. Ohime has never been to the dome's edge before. She's often looked up at the sky and seen the sharks circling above, but to be standing on one side of the glass with an alien world just on the other side is something entirely new to her. She reaches out her hand to touch the side of the dome. The glass is cold and she feels a slight vibration. Ohime steps closer to the glass and puts her nose up to it. Her breath forms a foggy circle on its surface. On the other side of the glass a pair of eyes blinks back at her. Ohime, startled, jumps back from the glass. A walrus with thick whiskers does a back flip in the water on the outside of the glass in front of her and then swims off into the darkness as quickly as it appeared.

She turns around to tell Timbre about the walrus when her eye catches something sparkle in the distance. It's something metal, some kind of ancient structure. She squints her eyes to see it better. It must be the ship hangar. They are almost there.

"It's there!" Ohime shouts, running over to Timbre and Eugenia. She points at the ship in the distance. "Do you see it? We're almost there."

The clownfish people gather around her, their eyes following the direction of her finger. Ohime hugs her baby doll to her chest and feels a wave of relief wash over her.

***

The traveling party follows the curved edge of the dome and makes their way across to the ship in the distance. They are careful to avoid the pillow lava pits and plumes of smoke. They walk cautiously across the ridges in the surface.

"Hey, wait up," a voice calls out from behind Timbre.

Timbre turns her head to see a group of about nine clownfish people lagging behind the others. They are standing in the shadow of one of the enormous snail shells.

One of the people is wearing a marching band hat with a tall red plume on it. "Her foot is sprained," he calls out and then bends over to help a smaller clownfish girl who is sitting on the ground beside him. More of the clownfish people are spread out, not paying attention, wandering off and getting stuck between lava flows.

Timbre shakes her head and keeps walking forward. She doesn't have time for this kind of crap. She has spent all day trying to round up these clownfish and figure out how to make their way safely across the lava. *If they can't keep up, they don't deserve to make it,* she thinks. Then she hears a squishing sound.

"Ahhhheeeeee," screams a clownfish girl.

A tentacle is uncurling from inside the golden snail shell above them. When she sees the giant tentacle, Timbre runs and jumps over the lava fissure behind her to get over to the group. But just as she lands on the other side, nine more tentacles the size of tree trunks come spilling out of the snail, blocking her path. Timbre swings her head around, trying to chop her way through the tentacles, but they are covered in a gel-like substance that gets on her hair. Instead of slicing like whips, her tentacles sink into the snails like jelly.

The giant tentacles swipe two clownfish people up into the air with their giant suction cups. Then the tentacles curl back up inside the snail, bringing the people along with them, devouring their orange and black bodies within the creature's mouth.

Timbre notices that more of the snail shells are starting to extend their tentacles.

"Run to the ship," she yells, jumping back over the lava fissure.

"We can make it!" Eugenia cries out.

Everyone runs toward the glittering metal structure as tentacles slash at them from the massive shells on the sides of the dome. Ohime shrieks as an old clownfish in front of her is ripped away from the group and pulled up into a golden shell. One of the enormous snail-creatures slides off of the glass wall of the dome, blocking the path of several clownfish people. Ohime covers her ears so she doesn't have to hear their screams as tentacles pull them into hungry mouths.

***

They get to the old, rusting structure with far fewer people than they started with. After they lock themselves inside, they can hear the sound of tentacles banging against the exterior walls, trying to break inside. Ohime leads the way through the giant metal hangar bay with Timbre, Jaffa, and Eugenia following close behind her. All around them are twisted, snake-like tubes that extend from a platform down into the lava fields, drawing power from the heat.

It has been years since anyone has been to this region of the dome, but all the lights are still on, powered by the volcanic lakes beneath their feet.

When they see the ship across the hangar, all of their eyes widen.

"There it is!" Ohime says.

The massive ship looks like a giant conch shell, wide and spiky at one end, narrowing to a spiral point in the font. It is white with swirls of pinks and oranges. It radiates a purple light that glimmers across the walls and floor. Timbre can't believe her eyes. Ohime was actually telling the truth. All of the clownfish people laugh and hug each other, patting Ohime on her starfish head, overjoyed to discover the ship is real. Even Eugenia feels grateful. It was the right decision to put their faith in the girl.

As they reach the ship, Timbre says, "This isn't at all what I pictured."

"It's beautiful," says Ohime stroking the giant shell.

They go inside the ship to have a look around. The inside of conch shell ship is shiny. The smooth pink surface has been overlaid with silver and inlaid with turquoise, seashells and other gems. The clownfish explore the spiraling passageways of the ship, running their fingers along the intricately patterned walls engraved with strange stars and other symbols.

"I knew we could trust you," says Jaffa, rubbing Ohime on the top of her starfish.

Timbre counts the clownfish people as they board the ship and choose their seats, making sure there are only twenty or less. But she loses count as Eugenia bumps into her shoulder as she passes her in the aisle.

"Let's see if we can power this thing up," Eugenia says as

she goes toward the cockpit in the spiral tip of the shell.

Jaffa, Ohime and mini-Ohime follow her, leaving Timbre behind to count the passengers. Inside the cockpit, they look out of the front windshield to see the vast ocean beyond the glass hatch of the dome. A school of parrot fish swim by and Ohime waves at them as they pass.

Eugenia sits down in the pilot seat and examines the flight controls. She explores the steering mechanisms, the pedals, the buttons. After a few minutes, she thinks she understands how everything works, but there's one thing that confuses her. She has no idea how to turn the thing on. There is also an odd panel to her left that she doesn't understand. It is a multi-colored board with a bunch of star-shaped holes in it.

"Ohime," Eugenia says, "your parents didn't give you any instructions on how to start this thing, did they?"

Ohime steps over to the controls and looks at the odd panel. The tips of her starfish curl up as she concentrates. She runs her fingers over the panel sticking them in some of the star-shaped holes, then squints her eyes and shakes her pigtails.

"No," she says.

"Maybe there is an instruction manual around here," Eugenia says, as her eyes dart around the cabin.

Jaffa searches through cabinets along the walls as Eugenia tries to read small text on the control panel that has been mostly faded away. Ohime continues poking her fingers in and out of the star-shaped holes until Timbre enters the cockpit and calls her over.

"We need to talk," Timbre says to the girl.

They step outside of the cockpit. Mini-Ohime tries to follow, but Timbre pushes her back inside with the back of her foot.

"Listen," Timbre says, rubbing the clam shell that Ohime gave her between two fingers. "Remember how I told you that you could only take twenty people on the ship?"

Ohime nods her head.

"Well I've counted and there's twenty-one of us total," Timbre says. "We're one person too many."

"I'm sure one more person won't make a difference," Ohime says. "We can always squeeze in one more."

"It doesn't work like that," says Timbre. "I checked the diagnostics; the ship can only sustain life support for twenty people. To take a single person more would be condemning everyone's life. We can't take that kind of a risk."

Ohime looks around at the people on the ship. They are all laughing and shaking each other's hands. They all have big smiles on their face. Ohime can't fathom the idea of leaving a single one of them behind.

"But we can't choose who can stay and who can go," Ohime says.

"I think the oldest should stay behind," Timbre says, pointing at an old man in the corner. "He won't be of any use on the surface."

Ohime looks at the old man. He has such a bright smile on his face and looks so excited to explore their new world.

"There's got to be another way . . ." Ohime says.

Timbre shakes her head and Ohime looks down, ready to cry.

When Ohime notices the shell in Timbre's hand, her starfish points spring straight up.

"I figured it out!" she says.

"What?" Timbre asks.

"The controls!"

Ohime runs into the cockpit and pulls shells out of her crabshell purse. She shakes them around in the palm of her hand. Then Ohime starts inserting the shells into the star-shaped holes in the panel. Eugenia and Jaffa watch as she puts a cone shell in a slot, then she places a moon shell, a limpet, two olive shells, a clam shell and a lightning whelk down on the board. There is one slot left, Ohime searches through her purse, she doesn't have another shell.

"What is it?" Eugenia asks.

"I need a clam shell," says Ohime.

Timbre steps over to Ohime and hands her the clam shell. Ohime looks at it and then places it into the last slot. Then the ship's engine whirrs to life.

Eugenia sits in the Captain's chair and examines the control board, trying to figure out how to launch the thing. Then, just as she figures out how to get the thing moving, the engine gurgles and then turns off.

"What's wrong?" Jaffa says.

Eugenia taps slams the palm of her hand down on the controls. Mini-Ohime slams her hand down on the controls, too.

"We don't have any fuel," Eugenia says.

"What do we do?" Jaffa says.

"I'll go outside and figure it out," Timbre says. "Wait here."

Eugenia nods at Timbre, but Jaffa, Ohime, and mini-Ohime follow her, hoping to help her out.

CHAPTER THIRTEEN

As soon as they exit the ship, there is an explosion. The sound of metal clangs against the floor as smoke fills the other end of the hangar. Ohime squints her eyes to see through the smoke.

"What happened?" Jaffa asks.

Then they see that the front door of the hangar has been blown off. Dr. Ichii and his henchmen are emerging from the smoke, walking toward them.

"Ohime," Timbre says as the men approach. "I want you and Jaffa to fuel up this ship and then have Eugenia get you the hell out of here. I'll hold Ichii off."

"But what about you?" Ohime asks.

"Forget about me," Timbre says. "Somebody has to stay behind. It should be me. I don't deserve to go to your new world."

Ohime grabs her by the arm. "But you're a nice person! You *have* to go!"

"You're wrong about me, Ohime. I'm not a nice person." Then Timbre turns and runs toward the attackers. "Not even close!"

"Wait," Ohime yells, running after Timbre.

But Jaffa grabs her and pulls her back.

"Let her go," he says. "She knows what she's doing."

"But she can't stay behind!" Ohime says. "Not her!"

"She's giving us a chance to escape," he says. "If we don't figure out a way to fuel up the ship right now then she'll have sacrificed herself for nothing."

Tears run down Ohime's cheeks, but she knows Jaffa is right. She turns to him and nods her head. Then they go searching for fuel.

***

Timbre runs toward Dr. Ichii. The swordfish man steps into her way and slashes at her with the long sword protruding from his face. Timbre ducks and rolls out of his way. She swings her tentacles around and slices the sword right off his head. A fountain of blood spurts up from his missing appendage. He screams and falls to the ground, holding his face.

The halibut woman leaps on top of Timbre from behind. Timbre shoves her stiletto heel into the woman and she flies backward. The woman opens her enlarged fish mouth and strange regurgitating gurgling noises issue from her abdomen until she spits a giant glob of stomach acid at Timbre. Timbre jumps out of the way and the acid hits the metal launching dock, causing it to corrode and discolor. Before she can spit again, Timbre jumps up and twists in the air, releasing poison darts straight into her chest.

The woman staggers a little, but isn't paralyzed. She doesn't seem affected by the poison in the darts. The halibut woman smiles at her with teeth bigger than Timbre's head. Then she charges.

***

Ohime can see Timbre fighting the fish mutants as she searches the area for fuel. She can hear loud banging sounds on the ceiling and walls around her as the colossal snail creatures try to break through to get to them. The walls are holding, but they won't hold for long. This structure is very old. It's only a matter of time before it collapses. They have to hurry.

Ohime goes to Jaffa on the other side of the ship.

"Find anything?" Ohime asks.

"All I can find are a bunch of useless barrels," he says. "Most of them empty." He kicks one of the barrels, the sound echoes through the facility. "We don't even know what powers this thing."

Ohime looks down at the black hoses coming out of the lava and follows them with her eyes up to where they are connected at the top of the ship.

"Maybe it's powered by the same thing as the lights," Ohime says, pointing at the tubes on the top of the ship.

"You might be right," Jaffa says has he follows her gaze up to the black hoses.

***

Dr. Ichii laughs as he watches the fight between the two women.

The halibut woman punches Timbre in the stomach with her boulder-sized fist. Timbre hunches over her massive fist in pain, then elbows the woman in the kidney. Both of them separate, rubbing their wounds. Ichii laughs at them.

"Just kill the bitch," he tells his henchman.

The large women nods and then charges forward fists-first. Timbre jumps up and roundhouse kicks the halibut woman back into a wall and then slices her head neatly off her torso with one of her red tentacles.

The giant fish head flops off the woman's body and rolls across the steel floor landing in front of Dr. Ichii's feet. He looks down at the fish head, its giant tongue lolling out of her mouth.

"You always were an efficient assassin," Dr. Ichii says, straightening his spine. "Too bad you had to turn out to be such a disappointment."

He steps closer to her.

"I guess I'll have to kill you myself," he says, as two metal rods shoot out of his wrists and unfold to his sides into two long tridents.

***

On top of the ship, Jaffa and Ohime discover that there is a pile of debris that most likely had fallen from the hangar ceiling ages ago. The debris is stacked on top of the hoses, cutting off the power supply to the ship.

When Jaffa understands the problem, he says, "We're going to have to move this rubble off the power line in order to recharge the ship's fuel cells."

Ohime nods her head. "Let's do it."

They begin removing the rubble one piece at a time, tossing chunks of metal off the side of the ship. Jaffa lifts the large chunks, Ohime lifts the medium-sized chunks, and mini-Ohime removes all the tiny pebble-sized pieces.

There are a few slabs of metal that are so big that it

requires all three of their strengths combines to lift one. They save these big ones for last.

"Ready?" Jaffa says, as they gather around a mattress-sized sheet of steel.

"Ready!" the Ohimes say.

As they lift it, something whizzes past Jaffa's face and hits the hull of the ship behind him.

He looks up and sees the rooster fish woman shooting arrows down of him from the steel girder above.

"Oh crap," Jaffa says. "Take cover!"

They lower one side of the steel sheet to use as a shield and duck behind it. Freya releases another arrow and it hits the other side of their shield. The spiral shell arrowhead continues spinning even after it's hit its target, drilling through the sheet of metal. Ohime's eyes widen as the arrow grinds its way through, emerging two inches away from her face. As it makes its way all the way through, it whizzes past her head and then drills its way through the wall behind them.

***

The ceiling breaks open in four different sections, and giant tentacles enter the room, squirming through the air.

Timbre summersaults toward Dr. Ichii and says, "I've been looking forward to killing you for a long time."

Dr. Ichii spreads his arms out to his sides and the trident ends of his long metal implants spin like drill tips.

"You'll never have the chance," says Ichii.

Behind Dr. Ichii, on the ground, the swordfish man is still alive, struggling to breathe. He lies in a pool of his own blood, holding his massive head wound. As he sees

Timbre fighting his boss, he pulls himself to his feet. He picks up his severed sword nose and holds it out like a samurai's katana. Then he charges Timbre while her back is turned.

Just before he can shove the sword through Timbre's back, one of the giant snail tentacles reaches down from the ceiling and grabs him. It coils him up, suctioning his body, and then pulls him out the building. His screams fade away into the distance. Timbre doesn't even realize he is there.

***

Jaffa peeks through the arrow hole in the steel plate they're using as a shield, realizing the power of her weapon. But then he looks down at the ship they're standing on. He knows that if her arrow can pierce through steel, it could also pierce through the walls of the ship. The submarine won't last long if she turns it into Swiss cheese.

Freya jumps down onto the top of the ship, targeting them with another arrow.

"Wait!" Jaffa yells to her. "Don't shoot! Your arrows will pierce the hull!"

Freya sees the eyeball through the hole in the metal, points her arrow again and takes the shot. Jaffa jumps out of the way as the arrow cuts another hole through the shield, then hits the hull of the ship, skimming across the top of it and creating a narrow groove across the shell.

"If you put holes in the ship it will be of no use to any of us," Jaffa says.

Ohime looks up and see the tentacles tearing open the top of the hangar bay building like a tin can, knocking more debris down on top of the ship.

"That's not our only problem," Ohime says pointing up. The tentacles pry through the top of the structure, loudly knocking more metal off the ceiling. "I don't think she can hear you."

"We've got to lure her away from the ship," Jaffa says.

***

Timbre kicks Dr. Ichii in his fat barnacled belly with the flat part of her shoe, knocking him back. Dr. Ichii lets out a loud bellow and brings his long metal arms together in front of his body. The spinning tridents on the ends of his arms extend and retract, growing longer and longer with each extension. He swings his arms around, trying to stab Timbre with his pointed metal claws. Timbre moves quickly, jumps and dodges. She releases a volley of poisoned darts at him, but they do not penetrate his crusty barnacle-covered skin. She flies up and summersaults through the air at him, her red tentacle whips crackling like electricity.

***

Jaffa and Ohime run to the side of the ship, but they have to jump across to another steel beam in order to climb down. Below them is the lava with all of the black tubes coming out of it. They jump across.

Jaffa says to Ohime, "I'll lure her away from you, try to climb down while I distract her." And he runs in the opposite direction.

Ohime crawls across the metal beam, trying to balance.

Mini-Ohime clings to her back like a backpack.

Freya targets Jaffa again and releases her arrow.

The spinning arrow flies true and burrows straight through his shoulder, pinning him against the wall. He screams out in pain.

Ohime looks back to see the blue-skinned rooster fish woman targeting her next arrow at her. Mini-Ohime shrieks as the arrow flies past her head.

Freya runs to the edge of the ship and shoots again. The arrow misses Ohime's body but pierces her dress between her legs, pinning her to the side of the beam. Ohime reaches down to pull out the arrow and Freya releases four more arrows in quick succession. They pierce through her blouse under each armpit and to the side of each of her hips. She is completely stuck.

Freya comes in closer, aiming her arrow at the little girl's face.

***

Ichii runs at Timbre. His trident arms extending and retracting rapidly like pistons. She jumps straight up into the air and leaps over him. He stops, turns around and starts pursuing her again. Ichii's metal appendages extend out even further and the spinning tips of the trident fly off like throwing stars at Timbre. She spins to avoid it, the projectile flying past her face, between two of her sea anemone tentacles.

Then she cartwheels down the launching dock, dodging everything he throws at her.

"Get back here, you bitch," Ichii screams, frustrated that he's unable to land an attack.

***

Jaffa sees the roosterfish woman closing in on Ohime, but he can't do anything about it. The arrow is still holding him in place. He tries to pull it out of him as it continues drilling through his flesh, but it's in too deep. It has bored its way several inches into the steel wall behind him.

Several clownfish people peer out of the ship at him, and he waves at them to help, but they don't assist him. They assume he is waving at them to go hide rather than come help, so they disappear into the ship and hide under their seats.

Freya comes closer to Ohime and fires her arrow. It flies at the girl, going right for her eyes. But, before it hits her, Ohime's arm jerks up and catches it in midair. Her eyes widen in surprise as she sees the drilling arrow spinning in her hand, only inches from her face. She has no idea how she caught the thing. She just did it without thinking.

When she tosses the arrow aside, she looks up at Freya. The rooster fish woman is even more shocked at what had happened. She pulls another arrow out and fires again. Ohime catches this arrow as well, then tosses it down into the lava pit. Freya pulls out two arrows and shoots them at the same time. Even though they fly in two directions at her, Ohime catches one and then catches the other, lightning fast.

Both Freya and Ohime stare at each other with shock. Then Ohime pulls a cone shell out of her pocket. She looks down at it and smiles.

"How the hell did you do that, kid?" Freya asks.

"Shell magic." Ohime holds up the shell to the roosterfish woman. "Cone shells are for protection."

Freya shakes her head at the kid and sneers. She doesn't believe in any of that superstitious nonsense and thinks the kid is just messing with her. She feels her quiver to get another arrow, but discovers that she's all out. She drops the bow on the ground and draws a long curved blade from her back.

"Enough play," Freya says.

Then the roosterfish woman raises her sword and runs toward Ohime. But just as she steps onto the beam, mini-Ohime lunges at her ankle. Freya loses her balance and throws her arms back, trying to regain her footing. But mini-Ohime pushes her legs out from under her and she falls from the beam into the lava below.

Ohime looks at mini-Ohime. She gives her a thumbs up and mini-Ohime jumps up and down in triumph.

***

A piece of metal falls down from the ceiling at Timbre. She dodges out of the way, but it blocks her path. One of Ichii's spinning stars hits the chunk of metal and ricochets, grazing Timbre's back.

Timbre repels off of the obstruction with the toe of her boot and leaps backwards, landing right in front of Dr. Ichii. As she swings her tentacles at him, he catches one of them in mid-air and throws her to the ground. Then he smiles at her and stabs his trident straight into her stomach.

She clutches her abdomen and rolls onto her side. He looks down at her, his bulging eye stalks blinking rapidly.

"Time for you to die," Dr. Ichii says.

Timbre looks up at him and doesn't make a sound.

Then a giant tentacle reaches in from above and attaches one of its suction cups to Dr. Ichii's head. Ichii reaches out with his trident arms and stabs them into the ground in front of him. Then another tentacle warps around his neck and tries to pull him up, but Ichii's metal hands dig deeper in the ground, planting him firmly in place.

Timbre looks over at him. His eye stalks are filled with fear.

"Help me!" he cries to Timbre with a choking voice.

Timbre coughs blood at him.

"Get it off of me, you bitch!" he says, as the tentacle tightens around his throat. "I'll give you anything you want!"

The tentacle pulls harder on his head. His tridents carve deep grooves in the ground as he struggles to maintain his hold. His eye stalks wiggle frantically as the pressure builds inside his skull. Then his head is sucked off of his body as the tentacle tears it away from his silver suit. His body remains standing, propped up by the tridents, as a fountain of blood sprays out of his neck.

Timbre's limbs go limp as she loses consciousness.

***

Jaffa looks down at his shoulder. He screams as the drill-like seashell arrowhead finishes grinding through his flesh and comes out the other side. Free of his bondage, he pulls his bloody shoulder from the wall and goes to Ohime.

He helps the miniature starfish girl pull the arrows out of Ohime's clothing. When Ohime stands up and crosses the beam to safety, mini-Ohime leaps up into her arms to gives her a big hug. Ohime pets the tiny doll-like version of herself on the top of her miniature starfish. She smiles up at Ohime with her tiny purple mouth.

Jaffa and Ohime climb down to the launching dock and go to Timbre. She is lying unconscious, a flower pattern of blood beneath her eel skin suit.

"Timbre!" Ohime screams, running over to her, tears

rolling down her face.

Jaffa follows closely behind her. When they reach her body, Jaffa checks for vital signs.

"She's wounded badly," Jaffa says, "but she's going to be okay."

They pull her to safety, far out of the reach of the giant tentacles that are still exploring the room for more food. Ohime pulls some olive shells out of her crabshell purse and sticks them frantically to Timbre's wounded body.

"You wait with her," Jaffa says. "I'm going to get help with clearing the rest of the debris, then I'll be right back."

Ohime nods and he runs off. She holds Timbre's sea anemone head close to her lap. Mini-Ohime hugs her around the waist. Ohime looks up to see the headless body of Dr. Ichii across the room, still standing upright, like a barnacle-covered anchor at the bottom of the ocean.

***

Jaffa is carrying Timbre into the ship. As he pulls her through the door, Timbre begins to regain consciousness. She sees Ohime standing outside the door to the ship as the hatch begins to close.

"Wait," Timbre says, her voice is weak from loss of blood. "Wait, what's happening? What the hell are you doing?"

The door to the hatch continues to close with Ohime on the other side.

"No, you can't do this," Timbre screams. "She can't stay behind! I'm supposed to be the one. I'm the bad person. I'm not worth it. I'm not worth it!"

The door closes completely and Ohime disappears out of view as Timbre loses consciousness again.

CHAPTER FOURTEEN

Timbre regains consciousness as the ship's engines are whirring to life. Around her, the clownfish people are all strapping themselves into the seats on the ship. Timbre hears a loud noise and the door to the outside of the dome creaks open. Through the window she sees water spilling in from the ocean outside, flooding the lava fields and turning to billowing clouds of steam. Timbre looks around frantically for the starfish girl.

"Where's Ohime?" she asks. "How could you let her stay behind?"

Timbre runs to the hatch door and pounds on it, screaming. She puts her hands to the glass and looks outside. The boiling water level is raising higher and higher and the ship starts to float. She can't see Ohime anywhere.

Timbre runs into the cockpit and lunges at Eugenia, prying her fingers away from the controls, but she's too weak from her injuries to exert much force.

"We can't leave without Ohime!" she screams, as she falls to her knees away from the controls.

Eugenia ignores the woman and continues turning the

knobs, concentrating on piloting the vessel. The ship tears away from the power tubes and exits the dome into the wide ocean waters.

Timbre leaves the cockpit and looks out of the window to see the dome hatch closing behind them. She stares carefully through the dome glass to see if she can find the girl, but all she can see is a dozen of the giant snail creatures as they swarm the hangar, the walls collapsing around them.

Timbre falls onto the floor, crying. Jaffa comes over to her puts his hand on her shoulder.

"It's okay," he says.

Timbre whips her head around, her tear-filled eyes piercing straight through him.

"Why did you let Ohime stay behind?" she asks.

"She didn't stay," Jaffa says.

Her eyes widen. "What? Then where is she?"

"She isn't in the ship," he says.

Timbre looks at him, puzzled.

"Ohime knew there was only space for twenty people inside the ship," he says. "But she found a way take everyone on the ship."

Timbre is still confused. He points up, out of the window.

Then he says, "She's riding on the outside."

***

Outside the ship, Ohime the starfish girl has attached herself to the side of the hull. Her lolita dress has been pulled up to her chest to reveal thousands of tiny tube feet covering her belly, underarms, and thighs, allowing her to stick to the side of the giant conch shell ship like a starfish. The ship glides through the water and Ohime smiles at all the colorful fish they pass. Suctioned to the ship next to her, mini-Ohime has the same smiling expression on her face, wiggling her bare butt in the current.

Timbre looks through the window where Jaffa is pointing and sees Ohime spreadeagle, suctioned to the glass. The starfish girl peeks in at her—the points on her star sticking straight out in excitement—and gives her the biggest purple smile Timbre has ever seen. The smile causes Timbre to burst into laughter and tears at the same time.

***

The gilded conch shell ship breaks through the surface of the sparkling blue water and gently glides onto a white sandy beach. The sky is blue and the wind blows through the palm trees like a gentle whisper. The hatch of the ship slowly opens and Timbre steps out onto the sand. Her red tentacles curl and prickle with the heat of the sun. The wind against her red-swirl skin raises gooseflesh on the back of her arms and neck. She takes a deep breath and tastes the floral tropical air mixed with the saltiness of the sea. The warm sand radiates through the soles of her stiletto boots.

Ohime has already slid off of the top of the ship and is standing on the beach in the center of a circle of seashells, her dress completely soaked and covered in seaweed. Mini-Ohime lays next to her making a star-shaped angel in the sand by spreading out her arms and legs.

Timbre enters the circle and lifts Ohime into her arms.

Their eyes smile at one another. Then they both look into the distance, amazed to see what their world really looks like, above the water, under the sunlight.

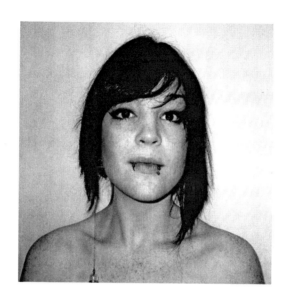

ABOUT THE AUTHOR

Athena Villaverde is a bizarro fiction writer from Toronto. She is a fan of kawii noir, fetish fashion, steampunk, Francesca Lia Block novels and Hayao Miyazaki films. *Starfish Girl* is her first novel.

Visit her online at www.athenavillaverde.com

Bizarro books

CATALOG   SPRING 2010

Bizarro Books publishes under the following imprints:

www.rawdogscreamingpress.com

www.eraserheadpress.com

www.afterbirthbooks.com

www.swallowdownpress.com

For all your Bizarro needs visit:

WWW.BIZARROCENTRAL.COM

Introduce yourselves to the bizarro genre and all of its authors with the Bizarro Starter Kit series. Each volume features short novels and short stories by ten of the leading bizarro authors, designed to give you a perfect sampling of the genre for only $5 plus shipping.

BB-0X1
"The Bizarro Starter Kit"
(Orange)

Featuring D. Harlan Wilson, Carlton Mellick III, Jeremy Robert Johnson, Kevin L Donihe, Gina Ranalli, Andre Duza, Vincent W. Sakowski, Steve Beard, John Edward Lawson, and Bruce Taylor.

236 pages $5

BB-0X2
"The Bizarro Starter Kit"
(Blue)

Featuring Ray Fracalossy, Jeremy C. Shipp, Jordan Krall, Mykle Hansen, Andersen Prunty, Eckhard Gerdes, Bradley Sands, Steve Aylett, Christian TeBordo, and Tony Rauch.

244 pages $5

BB-001"**The Kafka Effekt**" **D. Harlan Wilson** - A collection of forty-four irreal short stories loosely written in the vein of Franz Kafka, with more than a pinch of William S. Burroughs sprinkled on top. **211 pages $14**

BB-002 "**Satan Burger**" **Carlton Mellick III** - The cult novel that put Carlton Mellick III on the map ... Six punks get jobs at a fast food restaurant owned by the devil in a city violently overpopulated by surreal alien cultures. **236 pages $14**

BB-003 "**Some Things Are Better Left Unplugged**" **Vincent Sakwoski** - Join The Man and his Nemesis, the obese tabby, for a nightmare roller coaster ride into this postmodern fantasy. **152 pages $10**

BB-004 "**Shall We Gather At the Garden?**" **Kevin L Donihe** - Donihe's Debut novel. Midgets take over the world, The Church of Lionel Richie vs. The Church of the Byrds, plant porn and more! **244 pages $14**

BB-005 "**Razor Wire Pubic Hair**" **Carlton Mellick III** - A genderless humandildo is purchased by a razor dominatrix and brought into her nightmarish world of bizarre sex and mutilation. **176 pages $11**

BB-006 "**Stranger on the Loose**" **D. Harlan Wilson** - The fiction of Wilson's 2nd collection is planted in the soil of normalcy, but what grows out of that soil is a dark, witty, otherworldly jungle... **228 pages $14**

BB-007 "**The Baby Jesus Butt Plug**" **Carlton Mellick III** - Using clones of the Baby Jesus for anal sex will be the hip sex fetish of the future. **92 pages $10**

BB-008 "**Fishyfleshed**" **Carlton Mellick III** - The world of the past is an illogical flatland lacking in dimension and color, a sick-scape of crispy squid people wandering the desert for no apparent reason. **260 pages $14**

BB-009 **"Dead Bitch Army" Andre Duza** - Step into a world filled with racist teenagers, cannibals, 100 warped Uncle Sams, automobiles with razor-sharp teeth, living graffiti, and a pissed-off zombie bitch out for revenge. **344 pages $16**

BB-010 **"The Menstruating Mall" Carlton Mellick III** - "The Breakfast Club meets Chopping Mall as directed by David Lynch." - Brian Keene **212 pages $12**

BB-011 **"Angel Dust Apocalypse" Jeremy Robert Johnson** - Meth-heads, man-made monsters, and murderous Neo-Nazis. "Seriously amazing short stories..." - Chuck Palahniuk, author of Fight Club **184 pages $11**

BB-012 **"Ocean of Lard" Kevin L Donihe / Carlton Mellick III** - A parody of those old Choose Your Own Adventure kid's books about some very odd pirates sailing on a sea made of animal fat. **176 pages $12**

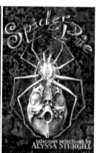

BB-013 **"Last Burn in Hell" John Edward Lawson** - From his lurid angst-affair with a lesbian music diva to his ascendance as unlikely pop icon the one constant for Kenrick Brimley, official state prison gigolo, is he's got no clue what he's doing. **172 pages $14**

BB-014 **"Tangerinephant" Kevin Dole 2** - TV-obsessed aliens have abducted Michael Tangerinephant in this bizarre combination of science fiction, satire, and surrealism. **164 pages $11**

BB-015 **"Foop!" Chris Genoa** - Strange happenings are going on at Dactyl, Inc, the world's first and only time travel tourism company.

"A surreal pie in the face!" - Christopher Moore **300 pages $14**

BB-016 **"Spider Pie" Alyssa Sturgill** - A one-way trip down a rabbit hole inhabited by sexual deviants and friendly monsters, fairytale beginnings and hideous endings. **104 pages $11**

BB-017 "The Unauthorized Woman" Efrem Emerson - Enter the world of the inner freak, a landscape populated by the pre-dead and morticioners, by cockroaches and 300-lb robots. **104 pages $11**

BB-018 "Fugue XXIX" Forrest Aguirre - Tales from the fringe of speculative literary fiction where innovative minds dream up the future's uncharted territories while mining forgotten treasures of the past. **220 pages $16**

BB-019 "Pocket Full of Loose Razorblades" John Edward Lawson - A collection of dark bizarro stories. From a giant rectum to a foot-fungus factory to a girl with a biforked tongue. **190 pages $13**

BB-020 "Punk Land" Carlton Mellick III - In the punk version of Heaven, the anarchist utopia is threatened by corporate fascism and only Goblin, Mortician's sperm, and a blue-mohawked female assassin named Shark Girl can stop them. **284 pages $15**

BB-021 "Pseudo-City" D. Harlan Wilson - Pseudo-City exposes what waits in the bathroom stall, under the manhole cover and in the corporate boardroom, all in a way that can only be described as mind-bogglingly irreal. **220 pages $16**

BB-022 "Kafka's Uncle and Other Strange Tales" Bruce Taylor - Anslenot and his giant tarantula (tormentor? fri-end?) wander a desecrated world in this novel and collection of stories from Mr. Magic Realism Himself. **348 pages $17**

BB-023 "Sex and Death In Television Town" Carlton Mellick III - In the old west, a gang of hermaphrodite gunslingers take refuge from a demon plague in Telos: a town where its citizens have televisions instead of heads. **184 pages $12**

BB-024 "It Came From Below The Belt" Bradley Sands - What can Grover Goldstein do when his severed, sentient penis forces him to return to high school and help it win the presidential election? **204 pages $13**

BB-025 "Sick: An Anthology of Illness" John Lawson, editor - These Sick stories are horrendous and hilarious dissections of creative minds on the scalpel's edge. **296 pages $16**

BB-026 "Tempting Disaster" John Lawson, editor - A shocking and alluring anthology from the fringe that examines our culture's obsession with taboos. **260 pages $16**

BB-027 "Siren Promised" Jeremy Robert Johnson & Alan M Clark - Nominated for the Bram Stoker Award. A potent mix of bad drugs, bad dreams, brutal bad guys, and surreal/incredible art by Alan M. Clark. **190 pages $13**

BB-028 "Chemical Gardens" Gina Ranalli - Ro and punk band Green is the Enemy find Kreepkins, a surfer-dude warlock, a vengeful demon, and a Metal Priestess in their way as they try to escape an underground nightmare. **188 pages $13**

BB-029 "Jesus Freaks" Andre Duza - For God so loved the world that he gave his only two begotten sons... and a few million zombies. **400 pages $16**

BB-030 "Grape City" Kevin L. Donihe - More Donihe-style comedic bizarro about a demon named Charles who is forced to work a minimum wage job on Earth after Hell goes out of business. **108 pages $10**

BB-031"Sea of the Patchwork Cats" Carlton Mellick III - A quiet dreamlike tale set in the ashes of the human race. For Mellick enthusiasts who also adore The Twilight Zone. **112 pages $10**

BB-032 "Extinction Journals" Jeremy Robert Johnson - An uncanny voyage across a newly nuclear America where one man must confront the problems associated with loneliness, insane dieties, radiation, love, and an ever-evolving cockroach suit with a mind of its own. **104 pages $10**

BB-033 **"Meat Puppet Cabaret" Steve Beard** - At last! The secret connection between Jack the Ripper and Princess Diana's death revealed! **240 pages $16 / $30**

BB-034 **"The Greatest Fucking Moment in Sports" Kevin L. Donihe** - In the tradition of the surreal anti-sitcom Get A Life comes a tale of triumph and agape love from the master of comedic bizarro. **108 pages $10**

BB-035 **"The Troublesome Amputee" John Edward Lawson** - Disturbing verse from a man who truly believes nothing is sacred and intends to prove it. **104 pages $9**

BB-036 **"Deity" Vic Mudd** - God (who doesn't like to be called "God") comes down to a typical, suburban, Ohio family for a little vacation—but it doesn't turn out to be as relaxing as He had hoped it would be... **168 pages $12**

BB-037 **"The Haunted Vagina" Carlton Mellick III** - It's difficult to love a woman whose vagina is a gateway to the world of the dead. **132 pages $10**

BB-038 **"Tales from the Vinegar Wasteland" Ray Fracalossy** - Witness: a man is slowly losing his face, a neighbor who periodically screams out for no apparent reason, and a house with a room that doesn't actually exist. **240 pages $14**

BB-039 **"Suicide Girls in the Afterlife" Gina Ranalli** - After Pogue commits suicide, she unexpectedly finds herself an unwilling "guest" at a hotel in the Afterlife, where she meets a group of bizarre characters, including a goth Satan, a hippie Jesus, and an alien-human hybrid. **100 pages $9**

BB-040 **"And Your Point Is?" Steve Aylett** - In this follow-up to LINT multiple authors provide critical commentary and essays about Jeff Lint's mind-bending literature. **104 pages $11**

BB-041 **"Not Quite One of the Boys" Vincent Sakowski** - While drug-dealer Maxi drinks with Dante in purgatory, God and Satan play a little tri-level chess and do a little bargaining over his business partner, Vinnie, who is still left on earth. **220 pages $14**

BB-042 **"Teeth and Tongue Landscape" Carlton Mellick III** - On a planet made out of meat, a socially-obsessive monophobic man tries to find his place amongst the strange creatures and communities that he comes across. **110 pages $10**

BB-043 **"War Slut" Carlton Mellick III** - Part "1984," part "Waiting for Godot," and part action horror video game adaptation of John Carpenter's "The Thing." **116 pages $10**

BB-044 **"All Encompassing Trip" Nicole Del Sesto** - In a world where coffee is no longer available, the only television shows are reality TV re-runs, and the animals are talking back, Nikki, Amber and a singing Coyote in a do-rag are out to restore the light **308 pages $15**

BB-045 **"Dr. Identity" D. Harlan Wilson** - Follow the Dystopian Duo on a killing spree of epic proportions through the irreal postcapitalist city of Bliptown where time ticks sideways, artificial Bug-Eyed Monsters punish citizens for consumer-capitalist lethargy, and ultraviolence is as essential as a daily multivitamin. **208 pages $15**

BB-046 **"The Million-Year Centipede" Eckhard Gerdes** - Wakelin, frontman for 'The Hinge,' wrote a poem so prophetic that to ignore it dooms a person to drown in blood. **130 pages $12**

BB-047 **"Sausagey Santa" Carlton Mellick III** - A bizarro Christmas tale featuring Santa as a piratey mutant with a body made of sausages. 124 pages $10

BB-048 **"Misadventures in a Thumbnail Universe" Vincent Sakowski** - Dive deep into the surreal and satirical realms of neo-classical Blender Fiction, filled with television shoes and flesh-filled skies. **120 pages $10**

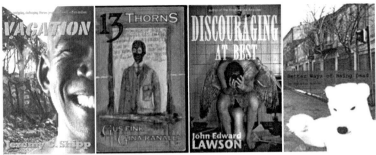

BB-049 **"Vacation" Jeremy C. Shipp** - Blueblood Bernard Johnson leaved his boring life behind to go on The Vacation, a year-long corporate sponsored odyssey. But instead of seeing the world, Bernard is captured by terrorists, becomes a key figure in secret drug wars, and, worse, doesn't once miss his secure American Dream. **160 pages $14**

BB-051 **"13 Thorns" Gina Ranalli** - Thirteen tales of twisted, bizarro horror. **240 pages $13**

BB-050 **"Discouraging at Best" John Edward Lawson** - A collection where the absurdity of the mundane expands exponentially creating a tidal wave that sweeps reason away. For those who enjoy satire, bizarro, or a good old-fashioned slap to the senses. **208 pages $15**

BB-052 **"Better Ways of Being Dead" Christian TeBordo** - In this class, the students have to keep one palm down on the table at all times, and listen to lectures about a panda who speaks Chinese. **216 pages $14**

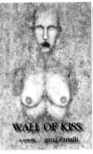

BB-053 **"Ballad of a Slow Poisoner" Andrew Goldfarb** Millford Mutterwurst sat down on a Tuesday to take his afternoon tea, and made the unpleasant discovery that his elbows were becoming flatter. **128 pages $10**

BB-054 **"Wall of Kiss" Gina Ranalli** - A woman... A wall... Sometimes love blooms in the strangest of places. **108 pages $9**

BB-055 **"HELP! A Bear is Eating Me" Mykle Hansen** - The bizarro, heartwarming, magical tale of poor planning, hubris and severe blood loss... **150 pages $11**

BB-056 **"Piecemeal June" Jordan Krall** - A man falls in love with a living sex doll, but with love comes danger when her creator comes after her with crab-squid assassins. **90 pages $9**

BB-057 **"Laredo" Tony Rauch** - Dreamlike, surreal stories by Tony Rauch. **180 pages $12**

BB-058 **"The Overwhelming Urge" Andersen Prunty** - A collection of bizarro tales by Andersen Prunty. **150 pages $11**

BB-059 **"Adolf in Wonderland" Carlton Mellick III** - A dreamlike adventure that takes a young descendant of Adolf Hitler's design and sends him down the rabbit hole into a world of imperfection and disorder. **180 pages $11**

BB-060 **"Super Cell Anemia" Duncan B. Barlow** - "Unrelentingly bizarre and mysterious, unsettling in all the right ways..." - Brian Evenson. **180 pages $12**

BB-061 **"Ultra Fuckers" Carlton Mellick III** - Absurdist suburban horror about a couple who enter an upper middle class gated community but can't find their way out. **108 pages $9**

BB-062 **"House of Houses" Kevin L. Donihe** - An odd man wants to marry his house. Unfortunately, all of the houses in the world collapse at the same time in the Great House Holocaust. Now he must travel to House Heaven to find his departed fiancee. **172 pages $11**

BB-063 **"Necro Sex Machine" Andre Duza** - The Dead Bitch returns in this follow-up to the bizarro zombie epic Dead Bitch Army. **400 pages $16**

BB-064 **"Squid Pulp Blues" Jordan Krall** - In these three bizarro-noir novellas, the reader is thrown into a world of murderers, drugs made from squid parts, deformed gun-toting veterans, and a mischievous apocalyptic donkey. **204 pages $12**

BB-065 "Jack and Mr. Grin" Andersen Prunty - "When Mr. Grin calls you can hear a smile in his voice. Not a warm and friendly smile, but the kind that seizes your spine in fear. You don't need to pay your phone bill to hear it. That smile is in every line of Prunty's prose." - Tom Bradley. **208 pages $12**

BB-066 "Cybernetrix" Carlton Mellick III - What would you do if your normal everyday world was slowly mutating into the video game world from Tron? **212 pages $12**

BB-067 "Lemur" Tom Bradley - Spencer Sproul is a would-be serial-killing bus boy who can't manage to murder, injure, or even scare anybody. However, there are other ways to do damage to far more people and do it legally... **120 pages $12**

BB-068 "Cocoon of Terror" Jason Earls - Decapitated corpses...a sculpture of terror...Zelian's masterpiece, his Cocoon of Terror, will trigger a supernatural disaster for everyone on Earth. **196 pages $14**

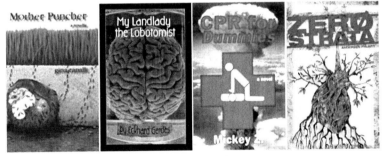

BB-069 "Mother Puncher" Gina Ranalli - The world has become tragically over-populated and now the government strongly opposes procreation. Ed is employed by the government as a mother-puncher. He doesn't relish his job, but he knows it has to be done and he knows he's the best one to do it. **120 pages $9**

BB-070 "My Landlady the Lobotomist" Eckhard Gerdes - The brains of past tenants line the shelves of my boarding house, soaking in a mysterious elixir. One more slip-up and the landlady might just add my frontal lobe to her collection. **116 pages $12**

BB-071 "CPR for Dummies" Mickey Z. - This hilarious freakshow at the world's end is the fragmented, sobering debut novel by acclaimed nonfiction author Mickey Z. **216 pages $14**

BB-072 "Zerostrata" Andersen Prunty - Hansel Nothing lives in a tree house, suffers from memory loss, has a very eccentric family, and falls in love with a woman who runs naked through the woods every night. **144 pages $11**

BB-073 "The Egg Man" Carlton Mellick III - It is a world where humans reproduce like insects. Children are the property of corporations, and having an enormous ten-foot brain implanted into your skull is a grotesque sexual fetish. Mellick's industrial urban dystopia is one of his darkest and grittiest to date. **184 pages $11**

BB-074 "Shark Hunting in Paradise Garden" Cameron Pierce - A group of strange humanoid religious fanatics travel back in time to the Garden of Eden to discover it is invested with hundreds of giant flying maneating sharks. **150 pages $10**

BB-075 "Apeshit" Carlton Mellick III - Friday the 13th meets Visitor Q. Six hipster teens go to a cabin in the woods inhabited by a deformed killer. An incredibly fucked-up parody of B-horror movies with a bizarro slant. **192 pages $12**

BB-076 "Rampaging Fuckers of Everything on the Crazy Shitting Planet of the Vomit At smosphere" Mykle Hansen - 3 bizarro satires. Monster Cocks, Journey to the Center of Agnes Cuddlebottom, and Crazy Shitting Planet. **228 pages $12**

BB-077 "The Kissing Bug" Daniel Scott Buck - In the tradition of Roald Dahl, Tim Burton, and Edward Gorey, comes this bizarro anti-war children's story about a bohemian conenose kissing bug who falls in love with a human woman. **116 pages $10**

BB-078 "MachoPoni" Lotus Rose - It's My Little Pony... *Bizarro* style! A long time ago Poniworld was split in two. On one side of the Jagged Line is the Pastel Kingdom, a magical land of music, parties, and positivity. On the other side of the Jagged Line is Dark Kingdom inhabited by an army of undead ponies. **148 pages $11**

BB-079 "The Faggiest Vampire" Carlton Mellick III - A Roald Dahl-esque children's story about two faggy vampires who partake in a mustache competition to find out which one is truly the faggiest. **104 pages $10**

BB-080 "Sky Tongues" Gina Ranalli - The autobiography of Sky Tongues, the biracial hermaphrodite actress with tongues for fingers. Follow her strange life story as she rises from freak to fame. **204 pages $12**

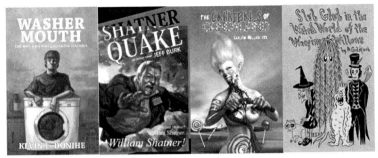

BB-081 **"Washer Mouth" Kevin L. Donihe** - A washing machine becomes human and pursues his dream of meeting his favorite soap opera star. **244 pages $11**

BB-082 **"Shatnerquake" Jeff Burk** - All of the characters ever played by William Shatner are suddenly sucked into our world. Their mission: hunt down and destroy the real William Shatner. **100 pages $10**

BB-083 **"The Cannibals of Candyland" Carlton Mellick III** - There exists a race of cannibals that are made of candy. They live in an underground world made out of candy. One man has dedicated his life to killing them all. **170 pages $11**

BB-084 **"Slub Glub in the Weird World of the Weeping Willows"**
Andrew Goldfarb - The charming tale of a blue glob named Slub Glub who helps the weeping willows whose tears are flooding the earth. There are also hyenas, ghosts, and a voodoo priest **100 pages $10**

BB-085 **"Super Fetus" Adam Pepper** - Try to abort this fetus and he'll kick your ass! **104 pages $10**

BB-086 **"Fistful of Feet" Jordan Krall** - A bizarro tribute to spaghetti westerns, featuring Cthulhu-worshipping Indians, a woman with four feet, a crazed gunman who is obsessed with sucking on candy, Syphilis-ridden mutants, sexually transmitted tattoos, and a house devoted to the freakiest fetishes. **228 pages $12**

BB-087 **"Ass Goblins of Auschwitz" Cameron Pierce** - It's Monty Python meets Nazi exploitation in a surreal nightmare as can only be imagined by Bizarro author Cameron Pierce. **104 pages $10**

BB-088 **"Silent Weapons for Quiet Wars" Cody Goodfellow** - "This is high-end psychological surrealist horror meets bottom-feeding low-life crime in a techno-thrilling science fiction world full of Lovecraft and magic..." -John Skipp **212 pages $12**

BB-089 "Warrior Wolf Women of the Wasteland" Carlton Mellick III
Road Warrior Werewolves versus McDonaldland Mutants...post-apocalyptic fiction has never been quite like this. **316 pages $13**

BB-090 "Cursed" Jeremy C Shipp - The story of a group of characters who believe they are cursed and attempt to figure out who cursed them and why. A tale of stylish absurdism and suspenseful horror. **218 pages $15**

BB-091 "Super Giant Monster Time" Jeff Burk - A tribute to choose your own adventures and Godzilla movies. Will you escape the giant monsters that are rampaging the fuck out of your city and shit? Or will you join the mob of alien-controlled punk rockers causing chaos in the streets? What happens next depends on you. **188 pages $12**

BB-092 "Perfect Union" Cody Goodfellow - "Cronenberg's THE FLY on a grand scale: human/insect gene-spliced body horror, where the human hive politics are as shocking as the gore." -John Skipp. **272 pages $13**

BB-093 "Sunset with a Beard" Carlton Mellick III - 14 stories of surreal science fiction. **200 pages $12**

BB-094 "My Fake War" Andersen Prunty - The absurd tale of an unlikely soldier forced to fight a war that, quite possibly, does not exist. It's Rambo meets Waiting for Godot in this subversive satire of American values and the scope of the human imagination. **128 pages $11**

BB-095"Lost in Cat Brain Land" Cameron Pierce - Sad stories from a surreal world. A fascist mustache, the ghost of Franz Kafka, a desert inside a dead cat. Primordial entities mourn the death of their child. The desperate serve tea to mysterious creatures. A hopeless romantic falls in love with a pterodactyl. And much more. **152 pages $11**

BB-096 "The Kobold Wizard's Dildo of Enlightenment +2" Carlton Mellick III - A Dungeons and Dragons parody about a group of people who learn they are only made up characters in an AD&D campaign and must find a way to resist their nerdy teenaged players and retarded dungeon master in order to survive. **232 pages $12**

BB-097 **"My Heart Said No, but the Camera Crew Said Yes!" Bradley Sands** - A collection of short stories that are crammed with the delightfully odd and the scurrilously silly. **140 pages $13**

BB-098 **"A Hundred Horrible Sorrows of Ogner Stump" Andrew Goldfarb** - Goldfarb's acclaimed comic series. A magical and weird journey into the horrors of everyday life. **164 pages $11**

BB-099 **"Pickled Apocalypse of Pancake Island" Cameron Pierce** A demented fairy tale about a pickle, a pancake, and the apocalypse. **102 pages $8**

BB-100 **"Slag Attack" Andersen Prunty** - Slag Attack features four visceral, noir stories about the living, crawling apocalypse. A slag is what survivors are calling the slug-like maggots raining from the sky, burrowing inside people, and hollowing out their flesh and their sanity. **148 pages $11**

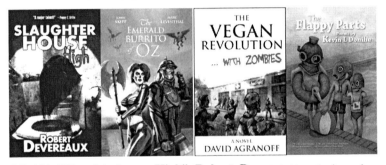

BB-101 **"Slaughterhouse High" Robert Devereaux** - A place where schools are built with secret passageways, rebellious teens get zippers installed in their mouths and genitals, and once a year, on that special night, one couple is slaughtered and the bits of their bodies are kept as souvenirs. **304 pages $13**

BB-102 **"The Emerald Burrito of Oz" John Skipp & Marc Levinthal** OZ IS REAL! Magic is real! The gate is really in Kansas! And America is finally allowing Earth tourists to visit this weird-ass, mysterious land. But when Gene of Los Angeles heads off for summer vacation in the Emerald City, little does he know that a war is brewing...a war that could destroy both worlds. **280 pages $13**

BB-103 **"The Vegan Revolution... with Zombies" David Agranoff** When there's no more meat in hell, the vegans will walk the earth. **160 pages $11**

BB-104 **"The Flappy Parts" Kevin L Donihe** - Poems about bunnies, LSD, and police abuse. You know, things that matter. 132 **pages $11**

ORDER FORM

TITLES	QTY	PRICE	TOTAL

ease make checks and moneyorders payable to ROSE O'KEEFE / BIZARRO
OOKS in U.S. funds only. Please don't send bad checks! Allow 2-6 weeks for
elivery. International orders may take longer. If you'd like to pay online via
AYPAL.COM, send payments to publisher@eraserheadpress.com.

HIPPING: US ORDERS - $2 for the first book, $1 for each additional book.
r priority shipping, add an additional $4. INT'L ORDERS - $5 for the first book,
 for each additional book. Add an additional $5 per book for global priority
ipping.

nd payment to:

ZARRO BOOKS
/O Rose O'Keefe
05 NE Bryant
ortland, OR 97211

Address	
City	State Zip
Email	Phone

CPSIA information can be obtained at www.ICGtesting.com
Printed in the USA
LVOW030227040112

262295LV00006B/78/P